CRY FOR DIXIE

by
Wes Scantlin

PublishAmerica
Baltimore

First printing

This is a work of fiction set in a background of history. Public personages both living and dead may appear in the story under their right names. Scenes and dialogue involving them with fictitious characters are of course invented. Any other usage of real people's names is coincidental. Any resemblance of the imaginary characters to actual persons, living or dead, is entirely coincidental.

At the specific preference of the author, PublishAmerica allowed this work to remain exactly as the author intended, verbatim, without editorial input.

ISBN: 1-4241-2891-9
PUBLISHED BY PUBLISHAMERICA, LLLP
www.publishamerica.com
Baltimore

Printed in the United States of America

Dedicated to my wife, Patti.
Thanks for urging me on.

CHAPTER ONE

My family was Irish. From all I know about them, they were a roughneck bunch. My Great-Grandad got here from Ireland just in time to get into the revolution against the British. He hated the British, and raised my Granddad to do the same. Grandad fought in the war of 1812, wanting to get in his licks at the British, too. After the war, Grandad moved his family down here to Tennessee, where my own Pa was born, not ten miles from here. It was way out in the woods, them days, and pretty much of a frontier. It's still pretty much out in the woods.

My Pa was a hard man, too. He loved to fight and drink, and when the Mexican war came along, he just couldn't wait to run off and get into it. He was gone from 1832 to 1839, and when he came home, he went back to carousing around. He drank and fought something fierce 'til he met my Ma. Then he settled down, bought this farm and worked himself like a mountain mule. He didn't care about anything or anyone except Ma. Yep, Pa was a hard man.

Pa's name was Padraic Ryan, and he was twenty when he ran off to fight the Mexicans, down in Texas. While he was down there fighting old Santa Ana, he was badly wounded, and a friend of his, named Taggart, carried him for miles on his back, 'til he could get help. Pa named me after him, and gave me a name that sounds like two last names. I'm Taggart Ryan.

Everyone just calls me "Tag" though. My brother, Jackson, was named after Old Hickory. We just called him "Jack."

I was the oldest, born in January of 1846. Jack was next, born in '47. Having the two of us boys so close together was too much for Ma, and with all the hard work, she was sick a lot and died when I was six, so all I remember of her is the warmth, softness, and the love I felt when she held me. When I think of her, the first thing I sense is the smell of baking bread. You know, kind of soft, warm and wonderful.

Pa didn't know a whole lot about raising little kids, and he worked us real hard from the get-go. I reckon he was raised that way, too, and just didn't know any better. Hard work, hard words and hard hands was all Pa seemed to be made of. After Ma died, he like to worked me and Jack to death. 'Course, he worked like that, too. Ma had left her mark on him, though, for she was somebody, them days. Her Pa was a doctor in town, and was well thought of and was well off, too. He doctored animals and humans both. Because of her, Pa was big on neat and clean.

Our whole farm was in first class shape, and we were, too. Pa kept us clean and neat, and saw that we ate right. We learned to say our prayers and to respect our elders. Another thing he did was have a young woman come in three times a week to teach us our lessons. Miss Ball was her name, and I thought I was in love with her. I used to dream about growing up and marrying Miss Ball. I didn't realize it until years later that Pa might have had something going there. I reckon that's the reason she kept coming around for so many years and putting up with me and Jack. I took right to learning, but Jack didn't like schooling atall. I reckon I liked the learning because of the crush I had on Miss Ball.

Jack and I rolled out of bed every morning at sunrise. Pa saw to that. We had chores to do. I milked the cow, fed the mules and Pa's horses and hitched the mules to whatever implement we would be using that day. Jack took care of the pigs and chickens and such, and then we would have breakfast, which Pa fixed. After breakfast, we all went to the fields. Pa and Jack to work tobacco or some other crop, and me to clear brush or break ground. I spent my whole childhood looking at the hind end of a skinny mountain mule. Life wasn't all bad, though. We got our first squirrel rifles when I was seven and Jack six. We learned to hunt and fish real early, and Pa would sometimes leave me and Jack out in the woods alone for a day or two so's we would learn not to be scared. We got to be real good in the woods, and Pa saw to it that we didn't fear anything. Like the Good Book says, "Not height, nor depth, nor any other creature." Only thing we feared was Pa. Pa saw to that, too.

Miss Ball had a younger brother, name of Thad, that was my age. Thad was the only close friend that Jack and I had. He was just as wild as we were, so we got along real well. We didn't have much money, us boys, 'course we didn't need much. A penny now and again for some candy and some change for powder and shot was all we needed. Pa traded for just about everything we needed. We raised our food, and our clothes were made by womenfolk in the area, homespun, don't you know.

Like I said, Pa traded for most everything, and one year, when some Cherokees came through, he traded a cow and a young mule for two ponies for me and Jack. Them ponies were meaner than sin, and only green broke, but me and Jack thought they were wonderful. Them Cherokees probably stole the ponies somewhere, but that didn't bother Pa. Thad's Pa and our Pa helped us finish breaking the ponies and they turned out to be pretty good saddle horses.

We feared Pa, and no mistake. He was a hard man and heavy handed when you got out of line. Our fear of Pa is what made us so sneaky when we decided the time had come for us to leave home. I disremember whose idea it was to run off, but that's what we allowed that we'd do. Like most boys, we figured that every kid in the world had it better than we did. We felt used and abused and felt like everyone thought we were just kids, and not to be taken seriously. Just like all kids. As a matter of fact, we didn't see ourselves as kids at all. Thad and I were fifteen, and Jack was fourteen. Mountain boys mature early. I reckon it has to do with hard work and a hard life. Anyway, the war had been going on for a year, and the South was purely putting a big hurt on the damnyankees.

A lot of the men from the mountains had gone off to the war, but some, Pa included, said "Thet ain't my dog in thet fight," and stayed home. None of us owned slaves, anyway, but most folks figured that the Yankees ought to stay up north where they belonged and stay out of southern affairs. Northerners were always good at telling everyone else how to live. Still are, for that matter. Us kids were scared that the war would be over with before we could get in on it. We didn't understand when Pa and some of the other Mexican War Veterans said that war was for young folks without a lick of sense.

We didn't understand about the sheer terror, hunger, and suffering that goes along with war. Why, the Confederate recruiters came through town in their fancy grey and yellow uniforms with plumes on their hats, real saddles on their horses and swords swinging at their sides and we thought it was grand. We boys wanted to kill Yankees and impress the womenfolk. We wanted to ride fine horses and be a part of the great adventure, too.

What we wanted most of all, though, was to get off the farm and away from home. Part of the reason we felt the way we did was that we were tired of the way our lives were being spent. We figured, rightly, that what we were doing day to day would be exactly what we would be doing for the rest of our lives. We didn't want to be farmers or backwoodsmen, we wanted to be heroes and have excitement in our lives. We just knew that life would be grand if we could just get away from here.

We figured that most folks were just like us, and we'd get along fine. 'Course, Yankees now, they ain't like us. Everyone knew they were devils. None of us had ever been more than a day's travel from home. We had never seen a big river, a city or a ship. We hadn't seen anything except mountains, horses, guns and hard work.

All that hard work, though, gave us hard, slender bodies with great endurance. None of us carried any extra weight, and we were as strong as young oxen. The mountains also bred independence. We looked and acted older than we were, but inside, where no one could see, we were just like any other kids.

I reckon that one of the reasons the three of us got along so well was that we were all similar, and all three different at the same time. We just kind of meshed with one another. I was the studious one that had to think everything through before I acted. The others thought I was a kind of an old lady most of the time. Thad, now, was just a good ol' boy. He was game for anything, and would follow along willingly into the direst straits. He was as near without fear of consequences as anyone I ever knew. He always looked on the bright side of things. I always expected the worst, so we made a good balance for each other.

My brother, Jack, now, was a case of his own. Headstrong and mostly foolhardy, he had no fear and no remorse for anything he did. He didn't care what any one thought. He believed in live and let live. If you didn't bother him, he didn't care what anyone did. The only values he had were loyalty and honor. Come to think on it, I reckon they are the only values you need. Jack's impulsiveness got him in lots of trouble, though.

Thad was a tall, thin kid with bright blue eyes and a crooked smile. Mostly good humored, he was a pleasure to everyone who met him. When he was little, he was tow headed, but now his hair was dark blond, turning brown. He had big hands ands big feet and we teased him a lot. Thad was my best friend.

I was an inch or so shorter than Thad, at five foot ten. I was a serious kid with a shock of black hair and brown eyes. I laughed a lot inside, but I reckon it didn't show much on the outside, for the others called me "ol' doom an' gloom" sometimes.

Jack, now, was the shortest of all, at about five foot six. I reckon that's what made him so aggressive and ornery. Short and skinny, with black hair and blue eyes, he looked like the "black" Irishman that he was.

It was summertime, and Thad and Jack and I were just a fretting and sweating to get away for a spell. We packed our gear and took off to go a cat fishin' down at the river for Saturday night and Sunday morning. We got down there just before sundown, built a campfire and just laid around watchin' our poles, smokin' our pipes and talking. The more we talked, the better the idea of running off to join the Confederate Army sounded. You know how young boys are; they can talk themselves into anything. Why, Good Lord, the war might be over before we could get in on it and be heroes. We allowed as how that couldn't happen, so we made plans to slip away from home. We planned to tell our folks that we were a going huntin' for a couple of days, so we could get a head start. No one would be able to track us down with a two day lead on them.

I laid there by that fire after Thad and Jack had gone to sleep just a thinking how fine it would be to be a soldier. I must have thought up about a hundred ways to die a glorious death in battle. Why, I could go out a hero. Then I thought that if I died, even like a hero, I wouldn't be there to see what kind of effect my heroic death would have on everyone else. I reckoned it would be best to live through it after all. Badly wounded, but alive. I just figured out lots of situations. Then I remembered that I really didn't like to be hurt all that much, neither, and finally drifted off to sleep thinking that maybe I could just kill Yankees and be a hero to the ladies.

When we awoke, the next morning, we made the final plans, agreeing that we would leave in three day's time, on Wednesday.

CHAPTER TWO

Monday and Tuesday, we slipped around and snuck as many belongings as we thought we would need out of the house. We were careful to not let on to Pa that something was up, and we did our chores same as always. I never knew that two days could take so long to pass. Finally, Wednesday morning arrived. Jack and I did our morning chores and then gathered our hunting gear and walked out to the barn.

Pa wasn't as dumb as we thought he was, by a long shot, for as we were packing our gear, he came out into the barn. He looked at us for a long time, then in his soft southern drawl, said, "Boys, be real careful, for there's been a lot of fightin' 'round here pretty close. I know yer not a goin' huntin' 'cause I seen ya' a packin' yer clothes an' such. I studied on keepin' ya' here, but I know I cain't watch ya' all the time. I know ya'll could run off if ya' had a mind to. All I can say is remember what I taught ya' and remember that ya'll can come home anytime. I want ya'll ta look after one another, fer yer all I got left of yer Ma."

Pa looked at us a while longer, then reached out and touched our faces. It was the first time we had seen our Pa show any kind of feeling for us at all. Kind of took us by surprise. Pa reached in his pocket and took out two leather pouches and handed one to each of us. He said, "There's a hundred dollars in Mexican gold in each of them. I brought some back from Mexico, an' we been real savin' of it all these years. I got some more, an' I already paid the banker, Flynn, to make sure this place gets took care of if somethin' should happen to me. I made a will, too. This place'll be here, so remember…ya'll can come home anytime." Then he looked at us again, turned and walked back toward the house.

"Pa!" I hollered. "We'll be back." Pa just took off his old hat and waved. Then he just walked into the house. Real strange. I reckon he loved us after all.

I looked over at Jack and saw that his eyes were full of tears. "Jack," says I, "if ya turn sissy on me now, I'll black yer eye."

"I ain't cryin', an' I just might black yer's. You ain't that much bigger'n me no more," he gritted.

I sure didn't want Jack to know that I felt as bad as he did. I couldn't let him see me turn sissy neither, so I turned away and finished stuffing my gear in two sacks. Jack finished, too, and we threw our sacks over the ponies' withers. We didn't have saddles, nor bridles, either. Them ponies were Indian ponies and never had a bit in their mouths. We just tied a thong around their lower jaws and only rode with one rein, just like the Indians. Another thing about Indian ponies is that you mount from the right side instead of the left. Indians don't mount from the left and them mean little ponies would kick your lights out.

Me and Jack, we rode down past the house and on down the lane toward Thad's place. We didn't look back for fear that we'd change our minds.

We picked up Thad in front of his place and started riding south on the road. We would leave the road in a few miles and head off across country. Thad was as quiet as Jack and I were.

I don't guess he felt much better than we did. Matter of fact, we all three felt as low as a lizard's belly and flatter'n a squaw's track. Leaving home ain't too easy when you're fifteen, even when you think you're chasing some big adventure. Leaves you kind of hollow in the middle, don't you know.

We rode south and west for the rest of the day, and about an hour before sundown, we made camp by a little creek. The woods were thick thereabouts, and a prettier sight you never did see. If you have never been in the south in the summertime, you don't know about the soft, warm, southern summer evenings. It's real still, and so quiet you can hear yourself breathe. Just at twilight, the lightning bugs begin to blink with a soft, faint green glimmer. The crickets start to chirp, one at a time, until there's a whole chorus of them. One by one the frogs start to croak their evening song and before long, there's a whole orchestra of natures sounds, all blended by the hand of Someone far greater than we are.

Thad gathered up some wood and started a little fire while Jack and I took the horses down to the creek and watered them. After they drank their fill, we rubbed them down with handfuls of dried grass. We picketed them just outside the light from the fire, and by the time we were through, Thad had put on some water to boil for coffee, and had whipped up some pan bread made from cornmeal. We fried some bacon and sat down to eat.

We still hadn't had too much to say, and after eating, we rolled out our blankets and sat down on them and lit up our pipes to have a smoke. Just about everyone we knew smoked, those days. Thad had a clay pipe, but me and Jack, we just had corn cobs. Pa sometimes rolled cigarillos. He brought back lots of habits from Mexico and Texas.

After we had smoked a while in silence, Thad took a poke out of his pocket and counted out three piles of gold coins and a few silver ones. Each pile had thirty three dollars in it. "Pa give me this money," he told us. "He knowed what we was up to. I wanna divvy it up with ya'll, 'fore I lose it. I'm a keepin' the extry buck fer myself." Thad murmured, "Pa said that when it ran out, we could head fer home if we couldn't figger out how to get some more."

Jack and I reached in our own pockets then and took out our pokes, and Jack said, "Our Pa said the same thing. You reckon them ol' goats talked it over an' did this a purpose?"

Well, I still wonder about that. Three hundred dollars was a sight of money, those days. Still is. Those days, three hundred dollars would buy a whole farm with all the equipment and livestock, some places.

We put our pokes back in our pockets, and Thad said, "Tag, Pa said me and Jack was a couple a' squirrels, mostly, but that you was mostly level headed. He said that you was to do the thinking. I reckon that's all right with me, fer I don't care one way or t'other. Pa said I was to give you some advice from him, though. You know he lost his leg after a fight with Injuns out west. He was out there for years before he came home. Well, he said for you to think on all them stories he told us about stayin' alive in a wild land. He said that this land is as wild as it gets 'cause of the war. Pa said that no one was to be trusted, and fer Gawd's sake don't ever let anybody know that we got some money. He said you'd know what to do, and to sharpen our knives, load our squirrel guns and keep our powder dry."

Now, mountain boys cut their teeth on throwing knives and hatchets. Most boys carried two knives, one at their belt and one in their boot. Me and Jack, we carried one more. We wore it in a sheath on a thong around our necks, hanging down our backs, or as I did, in a special pocket sewed in the back of the shirt neck. This was another of Pa's Mexican War tricks. Pa said lots of Mexicans did this, and it was a good idea for us, too. Nobody expected to find a knife down your shirt neck. We boys were uncommon good with rifles and knives, but we didn't have handguns, as a rule. They were just too dear for boys. A lot of the grown men had the new percussion revolvers, and some of the boys had old percussion and flintlock pistols. Single shooters. We didn't have any, though. Our squirrel guns were old cut down flintlocks of .36 caliber. You didn't want to shoot a bear unless you had a good, clear shot, for they took a long time to reload, and didn't have very much knock down power. They were good for squirrels, deer and men, though.

We checked the horses and moved to separate sleeping sites so that if we were sneaked up on, they couldn't catch us all at the same time. We didn't post a guard, for we weren't too far from home and hadn't seen any sign of them Damnyankees. I taken my horse into the brush with me, for I knew he would see or hear anyone before I did and his restlessness would wake me up. I could then watch his ears and eyes to see where the intruder was.

We kept traveling south for the next few days. Ever so often, oh, I reckon maybe twenty or twenty five miles, we'd pass through some little burg and ask where we could find some southern cavalry troops. We scouted them towns first, for it just wouldn't do to get caught by them Damnyankees. Everyone knew they were devils. We had seen some of them a time or two, and avoided them like the plague. It made for slow going, sneaking through the woods where only the game trails were passable.

In Storyville, we were told that cavalry was working over to the east, so we headed that way. We wanted to be in the cavalry 'cause it was a lot more grand than walking miles and miles with an infantry unit. Besides, we already had horses and rifles, so we thought all we needed was hats, uniforms, a sword and maybe a saddle. We didn't think about mounted drill, tactics, customs and courtesies and such. That type of thing never even entered our minds. There were lots of things we didn't know.

Reality was about to set in, though, and it would change our lives forever. Of course, we didn't know that then.

We had been gone from home for five days and were dirty and smelled like our horses, among other things. We didn't notice it so much, but when a lady in Storyville walked past us and held her little hanky to her nose and gave us a look like a bull gives a bastard calf, I took a real good look at Jack and Thad. When it occurred to me that I must look and smell a great deal like they did, I determined to do something about it.

The clerk in the general store made us show him some money before he'd let us look for some new clothes. I guess with our old dirty homespun rags, we looked like we didn't have any money. We each got some new canvas pants, a shirt and some socks. We bought some new long handles, too, which is long sleeved underwear that reaches clear to your ankles. There is a trap door in the rear for convenience. We decided to keep our old hats and boots, figuring that when we joined up the Cavalry would issue us some new ones along with the rest of the uniform.

We went back to the stables where we'd left our mounts and paid a little black boy ten cents each to bring us enough hot water for three baths. We surely needed baths, too. Horses, dirt and sweat get you right odiferous. We went ahead and threw our old clothes away. We were men of the world now, so we'd bathe in a creek now and again. We had supper that night in a hotel, and bright and early the next morning we rode east to find ourselves a war.

We rode all day, and never having been more than a day's

travel from home before, it was just beginning to dawn on us just how big this country really was. Southern Tennessee is mostly rolling hills with some really high, steep mountains thrown in for good measure. Anywhere you find a creek or a river, the country nearby is choked with brush and trees. There's lots of poplar, paw paw, some scrub oak, yew and a bunch of bigger trees whose names I don't know. In the mountains, some places the evergreens are growing as thick as hair on a dog's back. Brush fights with the trees for sunlight, and its real hard going to be off the trail here. Lots of meadows are in the rolling hills and they look like someone's pasture, many of them.

Tennessee is a beautiful state. No wonder that folks who leave keep a comin' back here. Everything was green. A hundred shades of green. 'Course us boys thought the whole world was green. We had only heard tales of Sonora's desert and the southwestern United States. We had no notion of the way things really are. Everything here is green. Different shades, but green just the same.

Along about an hour before sundown, we came across a bunch of wagon and horse tracks, and decided to follow them a ways, reckoning that we had found what we were looking for. When the tracks left the trail, we followed them down into a thicket on a ledge overlooking a big valley. Since we didn't know if these tracks were left by Confederates or by Yankees, we sneaked along real quiet-like hoping we would spot them before they saw us. We were riding along, fat, dumb and happy when from out of the bushes a loud voice hollered "HALT!" About then, what seemed like a hundred rifle barrels poked out of the bushes and pointed right at us. "Goddlemighty!" Jack screeched, "don't shoot!"

Well, when Jack screeched like that, my pony came unglued and threw me off. I hit the ground flat on my back, the wind knocked out of me and seeing little stars. Well, not really stars, for they were more like circles. As my vision cleared, the little circles faded into one big circle and that circle resolved into the muzzle of a rifle aimed right between my eyes. At the other end of the rifle barrel was a bright blue eye. I thought it must be the end of the world for me. Blue eyes looked sideways, spit a stream of tobacco and drawled, "Cap'n, I don't believe these here be Yankees. Leastwise none like I ever seen afore."

"I don't reckon," I managed to croak as I picked myself up off the ground.

One of the troopers had caught my horse when I was thrown, and he handed me the rein. I looked around for my squirrel gun and saw that I had fallen on it and broken the stock. With no way to make a new one, it was useless to me now. I had that gun since I was seven, and it seemed like I'd lost a part of me. I looked over at Thad and Jack and saw that they still had their hands in the air, and had dropped their rifles. It was then I saw that instead of the hundred rifle barrels I thought I had seen, we had only run into a five man squad. Still seemed like a powerful lot of rifles.

"Well," I thought, "we don't have anything else to lose since they caught us so easy. Even our pride is gone."

"Cap'n," says I, "we came ta join up. We want ta fight Yankees."

"Well," the Captain drawled, "I don't know about joinin' up. What I do know is that if we'd been bluebellies, yer fightin' days would be over just about now, Napoleon. You boys come along with me."

"Carlson," ordered the Captain, "gather up them squirrel guns and foller these boys back to camp. Sergeant," he continued, "you can finish posting them pickets by yourself."

And to us, "Come on, boys, an' don't drag yer feet." He

turned and walked off down a game trail. I hobbled along after the officer, leading my horse, for I didn't feel much like climbing up on him just then. Jack and Thad were riding along behind me, and Carlson, a blonde giant of a trooper, was bringing up the rear.

"Tag," whispered Jack, "I think I beshat myself."

"Shut up," I whispered back, "you want these guys to think we're a bunch a' sissies?"

Thad just sat on his horse and followed along. He was real quiet. The Captain, Clark was his name, led us quite a ways down that game trail, until we were almost to the floor of the valley. As we came around a little bend in the trail, some tents came into view. About a dozen, I reckon, in a little clearing, with about fifty more tents stretched a way back in the trees. We passed some sentries and headed toward a larger tent where a group of officers stood around talking. At least I took them to be officers, from the amount of gold braid on their uniforms, and partly because everyone else seemed to have a job to do. I didn't really have all the insignia memorized, so I wouldn't have known a lieutenant from a general.

Captain Clark walked up to a youngish gent, who seemed to be in charge, saluted, and said, "Colonel, we got us three infiltrators here, but I don't guess they're Yankees." He gave the colonel a wink.

The colonel turned to us and said in a deep voice, "I'm J.E.B. Stuart. What can I do fer you boys before I have ya' shot?"

Now, we knew a thing or two about J.E.B. Stuart. We knew that he had been a lieutenant in the Federal Army before the war, and that he was the one that took a company and stormed the building that ol' John Brown was a holding his captives in after his attack on Harper's Ferry on October 16, 1859. Stuart's commanding officer at that time was Robert E. Lee, himself, who was a colonel in the Yankee Army then. Stuart saved all eleven of the hostages, too.

What we didn't know was that Stuart was a real dandy and a fine figure of a man. He had flaming red hair, a bushy beard and piercing blue eyes. He dressed real nice, too. Just a lookin' at him a standing there made us want to join up that much more. Stuart wore a plumed hat, a red-lined cape, a yellow sash and a pair of silver chased Le Mat pistols. He had a flair too, though he was yet to prove it. We didn't know it then, but Stuart was moving east where the next month, he would give that Yankee General Pope a real lickin'. In August, 1862, Stuart would raid Pope's headquarters; take Pope's dress coat, $350,000 dollars in cash and Pope's dispatch book which gave the Union troop dispositions.

"Colonel," I says right quick, "there ain't no call fer that, Sir. We won't tell nothin' 'bout what we seen here. We rid six whole days just ta get here, a hopin' to join up with some cavalry. We don't wanna be no foot soldiers. We got our own horses an' guns."

"Well," he said, "your'n seems ta be broke. Cain't use no broke firearms. I'm guessin' the broke one to be your'n, seein' as how you're walkin' an' kinda dirty, like. Cain't use no soldier that cain't stay on his mount, neither."

"Colonel Stuart," I says, "that was a accident. Ever rider gets thrown, sooner or later, if he's a real horseman, an' I can fix that gun. I'll carve her a new stock, an' she'll shoot good as ever."

"How about us, Yer Honor?" piped up Jack. "Our guns ain't broke. We did want to stay together, though."

"Get down off yer mounts, boys," grinned J.E.B. Stuart, "an' come on in the tent an' we'll have a little talk."

"Here's how it is, fellers," said the Colonel. "Everyone in the south has a job to do right now. Ol' Jeff Davis, why, his job is to run this country. Bob Lee has to run the army and navy. My job is to make this unit of cavalry the best the world has ever seen. Captain Clark out there, has to run a small unit, a company, as well as I have to run this whole show. Some soldiers have to be clerks, some of them have to be teamsters, some have to be light cavalry, some have to be doctors and some have to be farriers, cooks or hostlers. See, boys, there's lots of jobs have to be done. You men know anything about farmin'?"

"Well, sure," Thad answered.

"So ya'll know how many jobs there are to do on a farm, right?"

"Yep," we chorused.

"Well," Stuart continued, "in the army, we have different men for different jobs. On the farm, one man does it all, and one skilled all 'round man is worth a dozen men working outside their specialties. I'll tell you what the biggest problem with this war will be if it drags on too long. We're fightin' on our home ground. All the good farmers are in the army or navy, and if we don't get this war over with in a hurry, folks will be a starvin' cause we cain't farm. If'n ya'll really want ta help, then go an' do what yer the best at, for if men like you won't feed us, we cain't fight. You got maybe the most important job of us all."

"Captain Clark!" he roared. Clark stuck his head through the tent flap.

"Sound Officer's Call and then come back here."

"By your order, Colonel," said the Captain as he left.

The colonel looked at us for a few seconds and then said in a soft voice, "I want you fellers to ride out of here the way you came in before daylight in the mornin'. The Yankees know we're here, and we know they're there, and tomorrow, I am going to roll up their flank like a big carpet. I am going to spank some Yankee behinds. If I live, before this war is over I am going to make my cavalry immortal. Historians are gonna be talkin' 'bout ol' J. E. B. Stuart's cavalry for the next hundred years or more. You mark my words, boys, I have the toughest, fastest, best cavalry in the world, an' I'm gonna do a big hurt on them Damnyankees."

You know what? He truly did. He was killed before the war was quite over, and he was only in his early thirties. He surely did leave big tracks in the history books, though. Just like he said.

Captain Clark came back about then and on our way out Colonel Stuart said, "Captain, these men will be our guests tonight. Give this one a .50 caliber carbine and some caps and ball. See that they're gone by first light. I'll see my officers in five minutes."

That was the last we seen of J. E. B. Stuart, but we heard lots about him for the rest of the war. We knew that he was just being decent, but he thought we were too young for service. He sure was right about that, as we would soon find out. None of us knew that by the end of the war there would be lots of fourteen and fifteen year old boys in uniform for the South. Things were going so well for the Confederacy in 1862.

Captain Clark came back from getting the carbine and took us over to a group of soldiers who were gathered around a fire getting ready to eat. He told them to feed us and keep an eye on us overnight. After picketing our ponies with the cavalry mounts, we got something to eat. We felt right proud to eat the same food as the soldiers ate. Cornbread, sorghum, beans and ham hock and real strong coffee to wash it down with. That coffee had lots of chicory in it. I still like it that way. We introduced ourselves around and sat down to look and listen. Pa always said not to talk too much and we would learn more. We learned from a grizzled old Sergeant named Mead that

Captain Clark was a descendant of ol' General George Rogers Clark of Revolutionary War fame, and was considered a good officer. When he gave orders, he made it seem as though you were doing him a personal favor. The men would have followed him anywhere.

We sat around listening to a soldier play a mouth organ. The men joined in the songs when they knew the words, and sang 'Lorena,' and 'Dixie's Land' along with a bunch of hymns for an hour or so before getting ready for bed. While we were listening, Sergeant Mead showed me about the carbine Colonel Stuart had given me. It was a percussion piece with a smooth bore and a twenty one inch barrel, so it would be fast to load while on horseback. Range was short, but cavalrymen didn't fight at long distances.

'Long about four o'clock in the morning, Captain Clark came and rousted us out of our blankets, and told us to get something to eat and ride on out of there. "Honestly, fellers," he said, "ya'll don't wanna see what's gonna happen down in that valley in 'bout an hour an' a half at first light. Ya'll go on home, now."

While we ate, we watched the soldiers. They were all quiet now. Some of them were checking their weapons a last time, some were talking real quiet, and some were praying on their knees. Looking back on it, I reckon most of them that weren't on their knees were praying in their hearts and minds. We didn't yet know what they were about to ride into. Somehow the reality of death hadn't quite reached us, yet.

We finished eating and got our gear together and went after our horses. Most of the cavalry mounts were gone, so we just threw our sacks over the horses' withers and jumped on. We rode real slow back the way we had come. We were all three kind of quiet and kind of sad that we weren't going to be a part of the battle, but a part of us, inside, was glad, too. Seeing those troops getting ready to kill and die had sobered us some. I wouldn't say it in front of Jack and Thad, but I was kind of glad Colonel Stuart had sent us away from there.

Us boys were about three miles down the trace when we heard it begin. It sounded like distant thunder and the roar of a river, far away. We hadn't seen the artillery positions and had not seen any infantry, for we had stumbled onto the flank position that Colonel Stuart had mentioned the night before. The Confederate Cavalry had been in position in the hills to hit the Union Army from the side in a surprise attack as soon as the Union was committed to a frontal assault on the Confederate positions.

CHAPTER THREE

We dismounted and sat on the ground for maybe two hours, listening to the sounds of distant battle before we decided that it was moving away from us. Finally, we looked at each other and Jack said, "I cain't stand it. I got ta know who's winnin'."

"Me, too," Thad joined in. "I'm a goin' back."

Well, that made it unanimous, so we mounted up and let the ponies run most of the way back to where we'd camped with the troops the night before. We slowed down and walked the ponies for the last little way when I reined to a stop and whispered, "Look it. Them soldiers might be a little spooked 'bout folks a comin' up behind 'em. Besides, there might be sharpshooters or sentries any place. Let's us lead the ponies to the edge of the valley and tie 'em up. If we get shot at or separated, we can meet back there."

We led them ponies for about another half mile 'til the trees and brush started to thin out some. Then we tied them up and went on down into the valley, sneaking along as quiet as we could. When we came out into the open, we stopped in shock and looked at the battleground with our mouths hanging open. "Lawd, have mercy!" Thad breathed. Me and Jack, we just stood there and stared.

I don't know if I can tell you what we saw and make you see it too, but I'll try. The valley was huge, and ran east and west.

It was a mile or a little more across, and we were at the head of the valley on the south side. The bordering hills were about a thousand feet high in places and dropped down to maybe a hundred feet kind of like the teeth on a saw. The valley itself was real green, but the hills around it looked almost black in the early morning light. There was hardly any cover on the valley floor, just scattered trees and brush clumped here and there like paint flung from a brush. It looked more like a big pasture than most mountain valleys do. There was so much smoke hanging in the still air that the valley looked like it was on fire. It takes an awful lot of gunpowder to make smoke like that, enough to blot out the summer sun until the morning looked like twilight.

Lying strewn around the valley floor were little clumps of things that resembled bundles of rags and logs, some lying singly, but most of them in little groups. Here and there, we could see quite a bundle of them piles of rags layin' around like broken toys. Them little bundles of rags, it turned out, were men and the little logs were animals.

Horses and mules stood, here and there, around the valley floor, with their heads hanging. Too tired and confused to run off, I reckon. We couldn't see exactly how long the valley was, for the smoke was as thick as fog, but in the distance, like ghosts, we could see a few cannoneers disappearing into the smoke in a hurry to chase the battle and get back into the fighting. Coming from down the valley, muffled by distance and foliage, we could hear some of the noise of the continuing battle. Under the smell of the gun smoke was another smell. Faint, kind of coppery, and slightly putrid.

Made me kind of queasy in my stomach. I hadn't known that battlegrounds smelled like that. I reckon most of us don't know that when lots of men and animals are killed the odor in the air kind of clings to the roof of your mouth and in your nose. Even sticks to your clothes, some. As I stood there taking it all in, a shiver shook my whole body. I reckon Captain Clark was right. We surely didn't need to see this happen.

Looked to me like the Yanks had charged across that valley and right into the mouths of the Confederate cannon. Then Colonel Stuart's cavalry must have hit them in the right flank and rode right over the top of them. The Yanks seemed to be on the run for fair, now. Bluebellies or not, devils or not, I felt kind of sorry for them. For each grey bundle of rags we could see, there must have been a dozen or more bundles of blue rags.

All them bundles of rags, blue as well as grey was covered with red, wet stains. I never knew a body could bleed so much. All around the men and dead animals were pools and clots of stain so dark as to look to be almost black instead of the red we always expect to see when we think of blood. Men and animals both had suffered horrible gaping wounds. Insides were sticking out of the bodies and many had arms or legs or even heads missing or mashed flat. Death on a battlefield just don't leave your body with much dignity. Here and there, lay a body that didn't look to have a mark on it. It was just as dead as the others, though.

Both sides must have taken away their wounded, for all the soldiers I could see were dead. The three of us walked a ways across the valley, thinking that if anyone was still alive, maybe we could help, but we didn't find anyone. We reckoned that sooner or later, after the fighting was over, someone would come back and bury all the bodies. I hope that was the way it worked, for you never smelled anything like it. Dead men, dead animals, blood and gun powder. Even after all these years I can't get the smell out of my head. Made a mark on me to last a lifetime.

We wandered back and got our horses and rode across the valley, just looking at the carnage. When we reached the other side, we started up into the trees where the Yankees had come from, best we could figure out. Never should have gone up there, I don't guess, but after what we'd seen, we weren't thinking as clear as we should have been. Home wasn't looking to be such a bad idea about then.

As we entered the trees, Jack spied a camp tent, a wrecked wagon and a bunch of gear lying around. There was dead Yanks all over the place, but we got off the ponies anyway, and checked them out to make sure. There were dead horses, too, and I didn't have a saddle, so I decided to help myself to one. These surely weren't doing anyone no good, so I stripped one off a Yankee horse and took the bridle too. I adjusted the bridle, put it on my pony and tossed the saddle up on his back.

I had just started to adjust the cinch to fit my smaller horse when I heard Jack scream "No!" and my side went numb and I heard a loud "pop." I didn't know what happened and spun around just in time to see a "dead" Yankee on the ground. He was pointing a revolver at me and trying to get off another shot. My turn is what saved my life. Without thinking, I grabbed the knife and I carried behind my neck and threw it at him just as he fired again. The shot hit my pony in the chest and dropped him with a sound like someone had dropped a melon. My knife took the Yankee in the throat. Since he was layin' almost down, it was a lucky throw. My whole body went numb then and I fell down beside my pony. I didn't know why I fell. I didn't realize that I had been shot.

Thad and Jack came a running with Jack still screaming. Only now he was screaming "Tag, Tag, are ya' dead?" My side was commencing to burn pretty good so I put my hand there and it came away wet and red. I thought I was going to cry. Then I remembered I had to be tough in front of my little brother and Thad. I sure couldn't let them see me panic. It's amazin' what you can do in order not to shame yourself. I was bleeding like a stuck hog, and I figured to bleed to death if we didn't get it stopped pretty quick.

"Jack, Thad," I said, "I don't know how bad I'm hit. Get some cloth to put over the holes and some of the canvas off that wrecked wagon to tie it with or I'm a goner. I think I'm shot clear through. See if there ain't some whiskey or something around here to pour in the holes. Horse liniment would be good."

Thad got a bunch of cloth from somewhere and held it over the holes until Jack came back with a bottle of something dark and smelly. I don't know if it was whiskey or not. I said, "Now, boys, I bet there's little strings from my shirt in that hole in my back. Try to get 'em all out before you pour in the goop."

Thad's hands were shaking pretty bad by then, but my whole body was starting to shake, so I didn't hold it against him that he was pretty rough tearing my shirt and getting the little pieces of cloth out of that wound. He finally poured in the brown stuff and it burned like fire. Anything that hurts that bad just has to be good for you. Thad held a pad in place and helped me turn over so Jack could pour the stuff in the other side. They wrapped the canvas real tight around my belly and laid me in some shade and put that saddle under my head. Thad found a canteen of water and fed me some, for I was powerful thirsty. Sick at my stomach, too, and weak as a cat. Time lost meaning for me then. I passed out cold.

I don't know how long I laid there before I came to, but the sun was getting pretty far to the west. I woke up stiff and kind of panicky because I couldn't move very well. I hurt and I couldn't see Jack or Thad. I needed a drink of water real bad and my face felt real hot. I started to call for Jack, but all that came out was a croak. They had left a canteen a few feet away, but it took me a couple of minutes to focus on it and get it. Took me some doing just to get it open.

Jack came back into view in a little bit. He had gone to get my knife back and clean it up.

"Kind of gave me the willies, getting it out of his throat," Jack said. "Can't believe he had the strength left to pull down on you. He was all shot up."

"Well," I replied, "he wasn't in his right mind or he never would have took us fer soldiers. I guess if he heard us talk he knowed we was not Yankees, though. I don't blame him for shootin' me. I'd likely done the same. Where's Thad?"

"Oh, he's down in the valley trying to get you another horse. I guess you forgot that old Spot got shot, too. We cain't stay here, Tag. You know what you said; that someone was going to come to take care of those bodies. If it's Yankees, they'll kill us sure. We got to move you. I guess we'll have to tie ya' in a Yankee saddle. I'm sorry, Tag."

Shortly after that, Thad came back leading a mouse colored gelding and told me it was to replace mine. I commented on the US brand on his hip and Thad said, "A Yankee shot yer horse, so Yankees owe ya' another one. I ain't about to steal a Confederate horse. While I was down there lookin' at them dead Yankees, I said to myself, 'Thad, you best steal two more saddles and bridles, too, for you and Jack ain't got one', so I took 'em. I took two of them pistols like the one you got shot by, for each of us. I got six of them and some leather holsters and two more of them carbines, too. Got us some lead and bullet moulds. Don't say nothin' 'bout stealin' Tag, this stuff was all owned by Yankees. I was real careful not to take anything from our boys. We got to move ya' now, Tag, we cain't stay here no longer. I seen movement way off down the valley. Someone is comin' back."

Thad had gotten saddle bags too, so they transferred all our gear out of the sacks we were using and tied them on the horses. Then Thad and Jacked helped me mount and tied me in the saddle. I passed out again almost as soon as we started out, and it was full dark, and we were in camp, when I came to again. I was layin' on my blanket and Jack had a small fire going. Thad asked me if I wanted something to eat but I couldn't do it, so I said, "No." Thad had a cinch ring that holds the girth to a saddle, a heating in the fire. He looked at me and said, "Tag, you're a bleedin' again an' we got to burn ya' to stop it. I'll have to do it I guess, 'cause Jack don't want to."

I just nodded to go ahead. Thad cut a green stick for me to bite down on, and stuck it between my teeth. Jack took the bandages loose and turned his head away. Jack's kind of soft hearted, you see. Thad picked up the cinch ring with a couple of green sticks that he had soaking in some water, and brought it over to where I was lying, and touched it to the bleeding wound in my lower left side. I bit down on that piece of wood, I can tell you. The smoke curled up and the burning skin made a hissing noise. It hurt beyond telling, and I went under again. When they brought me around, it was all over. They'd done the other side, too, and re-wrapped the wounds. Jack allowed as how the bullet 'didn't hit too many of my innards, else I would of croaked by now.' The entrance wound was just to the left of my backbone and exited in front, just over the hip bone. I still have some nasty lookin' scars.

I had bled a lot, so I was too weak and too sore to travel for a couple of weeks. When we saw that I wasn't going to be going anywhere soon, Thad rode into town and got an old, used tent and some food and a coal oil lantern. We just kind of camped out there in the woods. There weren't many doctors in those days, so a body had to tough most things out.

While I was laying there with nothing to do except heal, I started messing with one of them pistols Thad had taken off them dead Yankees. It was a .36 caliber single action six shooter. It was percussion, and we had plenty of caps. Now, it's quite a chore to load six shots into a small cylinder in a hurry, so I decided that after I could ride again that I would get me three or four more cylinders for it so I didn't have to reload so often. You can change cylinders real quick. I'd never messed with a pistol before, so I took the thing apart and put it back together again over and over and over until I was familiar with every little part, every screw and every spring. I played with that thing until it felt like part of my hand. I spent hours just popping the caps without loading any powder or ball until I knew exactly how much pressure was needed to set it off and make it fire.

After a few days, I began to feel more human, so I started to walk around a little. I got one of those military pistol belts and hung it kind of low around my hips so as to be below the wounds. Now a military holster has a flap that covers the pistol up. I figured that a man might never in his life need a pistol, but that if you only once needed it, you would need it real bad, and in a hurry, so I cut that flap off. Then I saw that you might need to get your finger on the trigger real quick, so I cut down around the trigger guard and angled the cut up to expose the hammer, too. Then I spent hours and hours drawing and aiming that pistol. The holster kept flapping around, so I cut a thong and tied it down on my leg. I didn't know that in years to come, lots of folks would wear this kind of a holster. I never would have made mine if I hadn't had to take it easy for a while. Anyway, I played with that gun for four or five hours every day, and in a couple of weeks could get it out and fire it right smart-like. I was to spend at least a half hour a day drawing that gun for a lot of years.

All the time I had been laid up, the three of us had been talking to each other a lot, and none of us wanted to go home. We talked and argued ourselves blue in the face trying to decide where to go next. Jack found a box with a whole bunch of

Yankee money in it in one of them wrecked wagons just before I got shot. There was a couple of hundred dollars worth of gold, which we had divvied up, but we had no use for five thousand dollars in Yankee paper money.

We thought about going up north a ways to find some place to spend some of it, but we were afraid the Bluebellies would catch us and kill us, so we didn't. We didn't want it to be found on us in the south, neither, for fear that someone would think we were Yankees. We just didn't know what to do with it. We couldn't spend it and couldn't make ourselves throw it away. We knew that when the South finished whippin' the Yanks, it wouldn't be worth anything anyhow. We just stuck it in a saddlebag and took it along. We finally decided to head on down to New Orleans. We'd all heard all our lives what a grand place New Orleans was.

CHAPTER FOUR

We figured since we weren't goin' home, that we needed enough gear so we could live in the woods. We had a lot of stuff that the boys had scrounged and bought while I was laid up that if we loaded it on the horses, there wouldn't be room for us to ride, what with the little tent, frying pans, coffee pots, food and such. I don't know how we got so much stuff so quick. We decided that we needed a couple of pack horses so our saddle horses wouldn't have to tote anything but the rider.

We saddled up and went to town. Thad and Jack had ridden their saddles a lot, but this was the first time I had sat in mine and it was real nice. Saddles are kind of slick and your pants slide around some at first, so it takes some gettin' used to. When you ride bareback, the hair kind of sticks to you better. If your horse has a bony back, saddles are a lot nicer, 'cause a bony horse back just raises Cain with your crotch.

We had no more than raised a trot when my pistol fell out of the holster. I kind of seen why they had that flap on there, now. I thought of just sticking the thing down my pants, but Jack and Thad were a laughing at my invention. They said that I had invented a little too much leather off of my holster. Well, that just made me more stubborn, so I looked around and decided to cut a little piece of thong off my saddle, punch a hole in the holster and let the pistol hammer down on the thong. It worked so good that I tied a little knot in the end of the thong so it wouldn't slip out from under the hammer. My pistol safe and sound, we rode on into town.

Now, a town of any size was a real treat for the three of us. We only had a half dozen shabby little buildings for a town at home, so Storeyville was a big, big place for us and crowded, too. The houses were cheek by jowl and the main street must have had twenty or so shops, saloons and other stores on it. There was a boot maker, a dressmaker, a carpenter shop, a blacksmith, gunsmith, furniture store (the furniture store was also an undertaker's place), a cooper and a general store or two. Why, this was a real metropolis. Must have been two hundred people living there.

Jack, being a kid, wanted to go to the general store first so he could get some penny candy. I wanted some, too, but I didn't want Jack to know it. I wanted him to think I was a man. After all, weren't we trying to get into the cavalry? Thad said he'd go with Jack, so, I asked him to get me some tobacco and some more percussion caps for my pistol. He said he would, and I went to find the livery stable to ask about packhorses.

I rode on down the street just taking in sights and lookin' for the livery stable. I noticed a man get up out of a chair and go into the constable's office. I knew what a constable was. We didn't have one at home, only a county sheriff. I finally spotted the stable and tied my horse to the hitching rail out front and went inside.

The owner was a little bald gent with a big handlebar moustache, a pot belly and the bowed legs of a man that must have spent most of his life a horseback. When I asked him about packhorses he said, "Son, I got a couple that might do you just fine. They ain't much, 'cause the army has bought up most of the horseflesh around here that was worth a damn. I'll make you a real deal on these 'cause they ain't good saddle horses."

We went out back to the corral and he showed me the animals. They both looked better than what we were riding. I said I'd give him ten dollars apiece, and he just looked at me like he didn't hear me right and said, "Son, them animals are worth fifty a piece or I'm a Chinaman."

"Well," I said, "I ain't ever seen a Chinaman, so you might be one. I'll give you twenty."

"Forty!" says he.

"Twenty-five." says, I.

"Thirty-five!"

"Thirty."

"Thirty-five is my bottom dollar," he finally told me.

"I'll give you thirty-five each if you'll throw in packsaddles and halters."

"Done," he laughed, and reached out his hand for me to shake. "Let's us go on inside an' I'll make ya'll a bill o' sale."

Just as we finished our business, we heard some commotion out front, so we stepped outside to see what was going on. There was a group of half a dozen people around my horse, and a fat man with a star on his coat was about to open my saddlebags. Now there wasn't anything of value in them, but that wasn't the point.

The way we were raised, a man's property was none of your concern. You respected his things and he respected yours. To go through another man's things was almost as bad as stealing, for you would be stealing his privacy. In our mountains, men had been killed for less.

To see that fat lawman do that to my stuff aggravated me for fair. When I get aggravated, I have a tendency to clench my teeth, and get real quiet, so when I talk, my voice sounds strange. Well, sir, I had my teeth clenched real hard and I gritted out, "Mister, when you look in that saddlebag, take a real good look, 'cause it's the last thing you'll ever see."

He looked over at me and said, "Don't threaten me, boy, or I'll give you a spankin'."

Well, I drew that pistol of mine and fired so quick it surprised all of us. I fired that shot right beside his boot. He jumped back and started to reach for his gun, but I cocked mine again and said, "That's the last warnin' ya' get. I'm too big to spank, and I ain't no boy."

He turned white and then real red and then puffed himself up and said, "You cain't threaten an officer of the law. This here's a Yankee horse. Look at the US brand on his hip. That's a military saddle, so for all I know you could be a Yankee spy."

"A Yankee shot my horse so I figured they owed me one. The Yankee that rode him ain't goin' to come lookin' fer him."

"All right then, I guess we're quits," the fat constable said. "Be out of town before sundown." He then turned and walked away towards his office. I guess he had to say that to save face in front of the town folks. He surely wasn't much of a lawman.

"Is that story you told him about gettin' that horse for true?" asked the stableman.

"Shore 'nuff," I answered. "Shot me, too. I been laid up the best part of three weeks. I know I oughten to have pulled that pistol, but I ain't feelin' strong enough to use my fists just yet."

I told him what really happened, because I didn't want him to think I shot a man just to get a horse. "Son," he said, "you was real lucky. The Yankees killed my oldest boy just before last Christmas. It was awful rough on his Ma. Truth to tell, it weren't so good on me neither. I tell ya what I'm gonna do. I'm gonna take that US horse off yer hands. I got a better one for ya'. I'm gonna trade ya' fer the horse I was savin' fer my boy. He ain't gonna need no horse."

"Mister," I said with a tear in my eye, "I cain't take yer son's horse."

"You'd be a doin' me a kindness," he replied. "Every time I look at that animal, I think 'bout my boy and it 'bout breaks my heart. This way, every time I see that US horse, I'll think about that Yankee that ain't goin' to come a lookin' fer him, and it'll make me feel a sight better, knowing that there's one less of them devils around to do a hurt to decent folks."

I took the horse. It was a good one, too. A sorrel with a blaze on his face. Stud horse. I would rather have had a gelding, but this sure was a pretty stud. I put my saddle on him while the stableman, Gaines, was his name, put the packsaddles on the other horses. I mounted up and rode toward the general store. I needed some new clothes for I had ruined my new shirt and long handles when I bled all over them. Got some pants, too. I figured that I might as well get some new boots and a hat, too. I was growing so fast nothing fit for very long anymore.

My bloody stuff had been burned, so the clothes I was wearing were a lot too tight. The pants were too short, too. Thad and Jack were sittin' on the boardwalk in front of the general store eating the last of their candy when I rode up. They gave me some peppermint sticks and some horehound drops. Horehound is my favorite candy. After they looked over the horses, Thad said he thought we ought to get another packhorse so we would each have one. I didn't tell them about the run in with the constable. Thad really liked that stud. He said that if I got tired of him, we could swap. I said I didn't guess so. Thad went off to see Mr. Gaines about another horse and me and Jack went shoppin'. Jack wasn't in much better shape than I was for clothes.

Up in the mountains, we didn't see too many new fashions, and we dressed differently than lowlanders. Our hats were made of felt and kind of pointy topped and the brims weren't stuff, so they kind of flopped down. Our pants were high waisted and held up by suspenders, and our boots were just ankle high farmer's shoes. Everything was made right there in the mountains and were so old that they didn't have any particular color. Everything was some kind of grey. Our boots had never been blacked, so they were grey, too. We didn't know the difference 'til we came to town. At home, everyone looked like us.

Me and Jack were still trying to decide on what duds to get when Thad got back from seeing Mr. Gaines about that packhorse. Gaines had told Thad that if he was with me, he could have the horse and packsaddle for the same money as I paid. That was real white of him, I thought. We each of us got a couple of new outfits. We got us some low waisted trousers, and them pants didn't even come up to our belly button, quite. Made us feel right stylish. We got us some belts, too. Never had had one, what with using suspenders all our lives. We each chose different colored shirts and pants, though. I favored a red and white checkered shirt and a blue and black one with black pants. Jack liked brown best, and Thad chose grey. None of us wanted blue pants, blue being a Yankee color and all. Our new hats were low crowned, stiff brimmed and cavalry style. We wore the hats, but didn't change the rest of our clothes just yet.

With all them new clothes, it just wouldn't do to be wearing our old beat up boots, so we went on across the street to the cobbler's shop for some new ones. Now, I don't know if you remember, but them days boots were made to fit either foot, and you didn't have a left or right boot. Well, we didn't know it, but cobblers had started making right and left boots, so that's what we got.

Looking back on it, they weren't a very good fit, but they were so much better than anything we'd had up to then, we didn't mind. The boots were black with high tops that reached almost to your knee, and you wore your pants stuffed down in them. The heels were a little higher than we'd seen before, but not as high as would be popular in years to come. The toes were pointier than our old boots, too. After choosing the boots, I left my gun rig with the cobbler so's he could dye it black to match. I was in love with that gun rig.

After all that, the barber shop was next on our list of things to do. I wanted us to get short haircuts, for our hair was near down past our shoulders. There wasn't any barber at home, so this was new to us, too. Out behind the barber shop was a bath house the barber ran, so we had hot baths. Afterwards, dressed in our new duds, the barber doused us with bay rum. Man alive, did we look pretty. Smelled pretty, too, for a change.

It was early afternoon by this time, and our stomachs were commencing to growl. There was an eating house down the way, and we started off to get something to eat when I got sidetracked at a gunsmith's shop that was on the way. What had taken my eye was a display of spurs the smith had in the window. They were real fancy, having come from out west or down in Texas somewhere, and I just had to have a pair. I wanted to hear the jingle as I walked, so I got a pair with big Mexican rowels. With my new duds and them big old spurs, I was so duded up that I looked licked to swaller.

I did have another reason for the visit to the smith, though; I remembered that when I had drawn my pistol, the barrel felt too long, so I left it there for him to shorten. The barrel was seven and a half inches long, so I had the smith chop two and a half inches off of it. Had him leave the front bead sight off, too. If I needed a sight, I figured to use my carbine.

Now, you know that young men and boys are always hungry. Matter of fact, they make a mama wolf look like a piker when it comes to eating. Eating at a nice place was real new to us, but we went on in the diner and sat down at a table that had a red checkered cloth on it. We had never eaten in a diner, but we knew how to use the tools, for Miss. Ball had seen to that. We didn't tie our napkins around our necks like some men do, or stick them in our shirt collar, neither. No sir, we unfolded them and laid them in our laps just like real gentlemen. Miss. Ball would have been right proud.

Back then you didn't order a meal from a menu most places. You just ate what they had fixed. If it was breakfast time, you got biscuits, gravy, meat, potatoes and coffee. Eggs, if there were any to be had. Dinner and supper were the same meal, served at different times. Dinner, to a Southerner is the noon meal. Westerners and Yankees call it 'lunch.' Bunch a' sissies, ya' ask me. Supper is what we called the evening meal. Anyhow, the meal was usually some kind of steak or ham, potatoes, vegetables, bread or cornbread, beans and coffee. Most times there was some kind of pie, and rarely a melon or a salad.

The little gal that was serving folks came over to the table and sat three cups of coffee down in front of us and said, "Show me yer money, boys. Food is right dear, an' these meals will cost ya' ten cents each." I showed her a paper Confederate dollar we'd gotten in change at the store, and she said, "I'll be right back with yer food, gentlemen."

Lord, Lord, she was a looker, I thought. Kind of chubby with dark eyes and hair and bright, white teeth and clear skin. She smelled like new baked bread. 'Bout five feet and four inches tall, I couldn't hardly take my eyes off of her. When she came back with the food, I felt my face flush, and looked down so's she wouldn't catch me a staring at her like that. My whole body was on fire, and when she smiled and turned to walk away, I could see that she looked just as fine walkin' away as she did coming towards you. I had never been much interested in girls before, 'cept Miss. Ball.

Jack looked over at me and said, "Tag, you feelin' alright? Yer face looks like yer fever might be comin' on again."

"We been goin' real hard since sunup," Thad opined, "maybe ya' orta go an' lay down somewheres."

"Naw," says I, "I'll be alright in a minute. Must be 'cause I'm hungry."

I sure didn't want them two to know that a durn girl could do that to me. They'd tease me somethin' awful. I sure was thinking about her, though, and didn't have much to say for the rest of the meal, neither. Jack and Thad noticed I was off my feed, some, but they laid it to my feeling poorly of late.

When that little gal came back to clear off the table, she looked me right in the eye and said, "I hope you fellers liked the food. I can see that ya'll ain't from 'round here, but I hope ya' come back."

"Well," I said, "I reckon it's the best food I ever ate. This is a right nice place. Not just the food, neither."

I was a lookin' at her like a fox looks at a hen, and she blushed prettily and went off to get us some more coffee. When she got back, I paid her for the meals and asked if she served breakfast, too. She told me that this place belonged to her Ma, and that she served every meal. I said that I'd see her in the morning, and she blushed again when she told me that she'd be there at six.

I had plumb forgot that constable and his warning to be out of town by sundown. While we were eating, we had decided to stay in the hotel right here in town instead of going back to camp. None of us had stayed in a hotel before, so we went and put our horses in the stable behind the hotel, turned them over to the little black stable boy and went in and registered. We took our saddlebags and carbines up to the room and laid down to rest a while before going out on the town that night.

After resting for an hour or so, we got up and went to look around the hotel and then went on out to see what was going on around town. First stop was the gunsmith's where I picked up my pistol, and then we went on down to the cobbler's shop so's I could get my gun belt. I strapped that black rig around my waist and checked the loads in my pistol. The pistol went into the holster and I let the hammer down on the thong. Thad and Jack thought it looked stupid worn low thataway, but I thought it was slick. I knew that if I ever needed it again, I could draw and fire quick as a wink of an eye. Let 'em laugh.

Any town was a treat for us, being from the hills like we were. Folks were a walkin' up and down the boardwalks and the women were wearing hats and carrying little baskets on their arms to hold the stuff they'd bought. We weren't used to seeing hats on women, for the women we'd known wore bonnets, mostly. Their dresses were ankle length, some of them, and now and then we could see their shoes peek out from under their skirts. The shoes had little rows of buttons down the outside of the tops. Real elegant, seemed to us.

Men had strange ideas about women them days. We were raised to see them as being a lot better than men were. Why even the thoughts of them having to do ordinary, everyday things like men did almost sacrilege. In our minds they were to be cherished and protected. I never could figure out why women wanted to be equal to men. I never to this day figured out why they wanted to lower themselves to our level. They've worked at it for a lot of years, now, but I do b'lieve they're about to get the job done. Damn shame, you ask me. We used to think they was right up there next to the angels. Nowadays, it's just our mothers and daughters that are in that category.

All the stores and shops were closing down for the night, and folks were a going home to supper, I reckon. A lot of the men were going in to the saloons for a drink, and a troop of cavalry had just come in to blow off some steam, so the saloon business was going full tilt. There was music and laughter coming out through the doors and now and then you could hear when someone won or lost at one of the games of chance that were offered inside.

Now Pa had told us that saloons were dens of iniquity. We weren't sure just what iniquity was, but the folks in there sure seemed like they were havin' a high time of it, so I don't guess iniquity was as bad as we thought it was. Matter of fact, it looked like so much fun that we were just a working up a sweat to get a little iniquity for ourselves, so we decided that when it was full dark, we'd see if we couldn't find out just what iniquity was.

After having eaten that big meal not long before, we weren't starving to death, but we thought we might like a little something, so we went into a little eatery next to the saloon and ordered pie and coffee. What it really was was an excuse to take a little more time to work up our nerve to go into a saloon. By the time we finished in there, it was pretty dark so we decided to look through the doors to all three saloons to see which one we would try our luck at. Now, we knew that unless the barkeep was in a good mood, we would likely get thrown out for being too young. There wasn't any law about that in those days, but if the womenfolk got up in arms about serving liquor to kids, the men folk would have to shut them down to keep peace at home.

The saloons weren't too far apart, all being located in the poorer end of town. I reckoned that to be to keep them away from where the homes were. I figured that the womenfolk might consider the saloons to be a bad influence on youngsters. Us boys, why, we got all sweaty just thinking 'bout getting influenced.

The first one we looked in was called the Planter's House, and was just too quiet for our taste. All the patrons looked like preachers, too, or maybe bankers, though we had never seen any bankers ourselves. Except for ol' man Flynn, back home.

The other two places both looked good to us, though. They both had a little skinny feller a pounding out tunes on a piano. The air in both places was full of pipe and cigar smoke and it was swirling around the lanterns that were fastened to wagon wheels suspended up in the air next to the ceiling. The places were both full of soldiers having a good time.

Townsfolk were buying drinks for the men in uniform and black coated gamblers were a running the games. There were cards, poker, faro and chuk-a-luk. One thing was pretty strange to us, though, and that was all the women we saw runnin' around. They had flowers and combs in their hair and had on almost no clothes atall. Their dresses were only knee length and barely covered their bosoms. Why, matter of fact, them dresses were so low that the women's bosoms, some of 'em, showed a crack between them kinda like a baby's bottom Made your throat dry just a looking at 'em. I figured all them dry throats was why the barkeeps sold so much liquor. The skirts a swirling around their bare legs just made a body want to go in, set down an' windershop.

Thad said it didn't make any difference to him which one we tried, so we picked the River House. There wasn't a river of any size hereabouts, so I don't know why they named it that. We walked up the steps and pushed open the doors. I'd never seen doors like that before. They only reached from your shoulder to about your knee, and weren't rightly any kind of a door atall. There was a table over in the corner that was empty, so we sat down and waited to see what we were supposed to do. A few of the men looked over at us, but most of them paid us no attention at all. I walked over to the bar, and when the barkeep came over, I ordered three beers. He took a look at me said, "You an' yer pals is too durn young ta be in here, Bub. Ya'll get on outta here, now. Yore Mama'll be wonderin' where yer at."

One of the gamblers walked over and said, "Sell him the beer, Charlie. If he's old enough to wear a gun and can pay for it, he can drink in here." Then he turned to me.

"I seen what ya' done ta our esteemed constable today. That took a lot a' nerve, fer a kid. Guess ya' didn't take him serious 'bout gettin' outta town before sundown. Don't be too surprised if he comes fer ya' tonight or tomorrow if yer still around. Don't get too drunk 'er too rowdy or I'll get Tim ta throw ya' outta here. Yer welcome ta stay as long as ya' want if ya' don't bother my customers."

I thanked him and took the beer over to our table and sat down to watch the crowd.

We just stayed at our table and sipped the beer. I didn't much care for it, but that's what the folks in here drank, if you didn't want rye whiskey. That place was really something to see. There was lots of noise, what with the laughing and shoutin' added to the piano playing. There was lots of them wicked looking women sitting on men's laps like a bunch a' tabby cats. Why, you just expected them to start purrin' any minute. Every once in a while, you would see one of them women walk up a flight of stairs with their arm around some man. We wondered what was up them stairs. Another saloon like this one, we supposed.

After a while, one of the girls came over and plopped herself down on my lap. "Howdy, Stranger," she lisped, "buy a girl a drink?"

I looked her over and she couldn't have been much older than we were. Had a lot of paint on her face, though. Kind of made her look a little older. She was right good looking, so I kinda looked down the front of her dress and said, "Yep, I'd be proud to."

"Excuse me fer a minnit, then, an' I'll find a couple of the younger girls fer yer friends," says she.

"Tag," says Thad, "I do believe them girls is hoors. I heard Pa an' them a talkin' 'bout women in big city saloons. They sell ya' favors."

"What kinda favors?" asked Jack.

"I ain't sure." Thad answered. "But I 'spect we'll find out 'fore the nights over with."

We stood up when the gals came back and all told each other our names. Kinda made small talk, don't ya' know? We sat back down and them girls sat down on our knees, us not having any extra chairs. They had an arm around each of our necks and was a playin' with our hair and such. Mary, now that was my girl, was about five feet two and had black hair and eyes. She was right slender, except for her chest, which was kinda plump for a girl of her size. Sarah, that was Jack's gal was a couple inches taller and had blonde hair. She was a sight too skinny for my taste, and flat chested, too, but Jack didn't mind. Eva, Thad's gal was a stone beauty. Curly brown hair, green eyes, red lips and she was built just about right, too. They all had on them short dresses so we could see a goodly amount of thigh and down their necks, too. We was in hog heaven.

Them gals just kept a bringing us beer and setting on our laps 'til I thought my fever was a comin' back. Jack was red in the face and blinkin' his eyes like a toad in a hail storm. Thad's eyes was bugged out, too. I couldn't hardly talk. We just sat there and let them gals put their hands all over us. 'Course, we was a touchin' them too. We hadn't never been touched like that before, and certain sure we had never touched nothin' like that before. I felt like I'd died an' gone to heaven.

We spent an hour or so with them gals, dancin' and whoopin' and a hollering. When we tired out some, and had come back and sat down at the table again, Jack blurted out, "We was a wonderin' if ya'll sold favors."

"Why, yes, we do," answered Sarah.

"What kinda favors?" asked Thad.

I wanted to know, too, but no one gave a good answer. Looking and acting like I didn't know what was going on wasn't exactly what I wanted to do. I was saved from making a fool out of myself when Mary leaned over and in my ear. "Take me upstairs, and I'll sell you a favor you won't never ferget fer two dollars."

Well, I just couldn't wait to see what these two dollar favors was, so I took her by the hand and we started for the stairs. My heart was poundin' so bad I thought I would pass out before I found out. We had just made it to the bottom of the stairs when the doors flew open and that fat constable hollered, "Hold 'er right there, boy!"

I had plumb forgot about him. He was a standin' there holding a sawed off shotgun and his face was red and hard set. I guess he figured to get even with me. All the noise had died down by now, and you could have heard a pin drop. Now, a shotgun is nothing to fool with, and I knew I couldn't get my pistol out before he cut me in two, so I turned to face him and meet my Maker like a man. I pushed Mary away and stood there.

"Yer under arrest," said he.

"You don't have no call to arrest me, Mister, and I don't guess I'm goin' ta let ya'," I replied. About that time Thad and Jack had sneaked up close enough behind him and Thad stuck his pistol right in that fat constable's ear. That man's face turned dead white as Thad said "Jack, reach around an' take the shotgun." Jack did it and I drew my own pistol. The man was speechless with fury at this.

"Boys," I said, "let's us go get our gear and horses. We'll take the fat man there with us for now. I should have shot him this morning. Maybe I will if he don't mind what I say." We marched that constable over to the jail and locked him in. Thad went to the hotel to get our gear and Jack went to saddle the horses. I waited in the jail.

When the boys got back, I had Jack hold a gun on the lawman while I tied and gagged him. We locked the jail house door after turning off the lantern and I don't know how long the man was in his own jail, because we never came back to Storeyville. We went back to camp and bright and early we headed west. I never did get to have breakfast with that pretty girl from the dinner house. Never found out what them two dollar favors were, neither.

We rode at a pretty good clip, just south of west, figuring to go west 'til we hit the Mississippi River and follow her south 'til we came to New Orleans. Not having maps like they do nowadays, we figured that we couldn't miss a mile wide river, and we knew that New Orleans was almost at the end of it. Ever so often, we would see a big house. Some of them were bigger than the hotel we'd stayed at. Most of them were white or made of brick and had these big pillars in front kind of holding up a porch, like.

We knew these must be the mansions we'd heard about. They were awful pretty. Fireplace chimneys on both ends and lots of windows and they had great big double doors. On the side or in the rear of these fine places were some small out buildings. One of these was usually the kitchen, located away from the main house, because there was always a fire burning to cook on and the people didn't want the heat in the house or in the servant's houses, neither. There was always a few cabins nearby where the servants lived. Sometimes there was a dormitory-like building where the field hands lived if they weren't "married" to a servant woman.

Now, I never paid much attention to slaveholders or slaves, and neither did anyone I knew. We made a habit of stopping every time we got a chance to around meal time, for we knew that most of the planter's would ask us to eat or stay overnight.

They were real hospitable, and most of them were real nice folks. The meals were wonderful, and we got to see a way of life that we didn't know existed. We asked all kinds of questions about plantations, slaves, the war and even planting crops and so forth. It was a real education. Most times, the fields were in excellent condition. Weeded, tilled and watered. We saw few signs of neglect. I guess when you have that much money, and have your whole life involved in the plantation, you pay attention to details.

I guess that owning people isn't right, because they ain't free to do or go as they please. They can't quit their job or move or marry whenever they please. I didn't see any signs of cruelty, though.

We had gone from home quite a while, now, what with my being laid up and all, so I decided to write to Pa and tell him that we were all right. We hadn't come too far from home when I got shot, so we crossed the Cumberland River skirting Nashville so as not to have to go into a big city. The real reason was that there was lots of Union troops around Nashville, and we wouldn't have been able to find a safe place to camp and all the inns would have been full. Fact is, we were too scared.

Anywhere there is an army, there are all kinds of hangers-on. People trying to get some of the soldiers' money, road agents and the like. None of us wanted the others to know we were scared to death of being robbed or shot by bandits. We wanted to be men, but we weren't hard enough, yet. Anyhow, we got back on the road at White Bluff and I wrote Pa a letter. When I mailed it, I had to explain where Red Boiling Springs was, it being about 50 miles, as the crow flies, southeast of Bowling Green, Kentucky. It being so small, the man at the general store didn't know where it was.

We rode out of White Rock at sunup and headed for Hollow

Rock. Now, Hollow Rock is only about 125 miles from home, if you could go in a straight line, but the way we had to go, it was a good four day ride for me, 'cause I still wasn't too chipper, and tired easily. Including the time I was laid up, we'd been gone 'bout twenty five days. We went on west to Dyersburg and then turned southwest to Brownville. We planned to lay around town a couple of days and rest the horses.

Brownville was a real small town in those days, and there weren't any soldiers there. We put up the stock at the livery stable and went to get ourselves a room. After we signed in, we took our saddle bags and carbines up to the room and went out to get something to eat. The only place in town where we could eat was right beside the hotel, so we went there. The town being so small, there wasn't a saloon or tavern, but there was a bar at the hotel, so we went in and sat down to have a beer. The barkeep said, "Ya'll are too durn young to be drinkin' beer. Ya'll can have a Sarsaparilla." This is what we had. It wasn't too bad, neither. We could see that there wasn't too much excitement to be had here, so we went on to bed and left the next morning for Memphis, which is where we planned to meet the river. Took us a day and a half of hard riding to get there.

We stopped at a plantation for the night, about a half day's ride from Memphis. The family that owned it was named McKenna and was as good of folks as there are. They wouldn't hear of us spending the night n the barn, but made us welcome in their home. It was a great big place and was a typical southern mansion. They had the servants get the guest rooms ready while we had supper with them.

Mr. McKenna and his wife were eager for the news of the war from the eastern part of the state, so we told them all we had heard on our trip and told them about meeting J. E. B. Stuart and about the aftermath of the battle that we'd seen. They said that they understood that war was awful, and told us that their son and grandson were both gone off to fight the Yankees. Their son had raised a company of horse and was named Colonel of it. They had ridden east a couple of months ago and they had had no word from them yet and were awful worried. We liked the McKennas. They didn't talk down to us or treat us like kids. They were real Southern gentlefolk. After supper, Mr. McKenna invited us into the library, as was the custom then, for an after dinner cigar and brandy, while Mrs. McKenna went about her business.

In the old South, the women left the men alone for this ritual. Mr. McKenna asked us if we smoked, and we said that yes, we did. He passed out the cigars, had a servant pour us all a little glass of brandy, and sat down to talk to us. He asked us where we were from and where we were going, so we told him the whole tale.

After he had heard us out, Mr. McKenna took a long look at us and in a strange tone of voice said, "Boys, I can understand ya'll wanting to be soldiers and kill Yankees because you see them as invaders and meddlers, and I reckon they are. However that may be, I want ya' to listen ta what I'm a gonna tell ya', an' I ain't no Yankee nor abolitionist, neither.

Up north, they work youngsters to death in their factories, so they got no room to talk about slavery. No, boys, this war ain't about slavery, it's about states rights and sheer jealousy. The Yankees want to make federal laws to pre-empt state laws on economic issues. They want to raise our taxes and lower theirs for they are under the misconception that all Southerners are rich and have dozens of slaves to do the work for them. Now, we know that ain't so, but most of them don't. For an excuse to fight, the Yanks scream about Negroes bein' equal, but I don't know a slave in the South that gets treated as bad as some so called free Negroes I've seen in the North.

I don't own any slaves any more, and I am one of the biggest cotton growers in Dixie. I pay every one of them day wages to work for me. I've put all my money in English banks for I know the South cain't win this war."

"Mr. McKenna," says I, "how can ya' say such a thing? Yer own son is off fightin', an' everyone says we'll whip them Yankees by next summer at the latest."

"I know it, son," says he, "but them folks ain't been up North and seen the factories and big cities. I know we been kickin' the Yanks in the crotch up to now, but the war ain't over, yet.

Folks like me will be alright when the war's over, because of our foreign investments. I'll try to give my neighbors a hand then, if I can. Lord have mercy, but they'd think I was a traitor for sure if'n they was to hear me a talkin' this way, but it's still a free country, fer as I know."

"Ya'll best turn in now," said Mr. McKenna, "and we'll talk some more in the mornin'. There's some things I want to tell ya' 'fore ya' ride on."

Mr. McKenna had his servants show us to our rooms. The guest bedrooms were good sized, with a view of the creek and servant's quarters. The floor were of polished wood and throw rugs scattered here and there, and each room had a 'sitting' area with a small couch, a chiffonier, and a table with a wash basin and pitcher of water, along with a drinking glass and hand towels. My windows were covered by drapes underneath. My room was Kelly green in drapes and upholstery with pale green walls. I had never seen such riches. The rooms had connecting doors and were each done in a different color scheme. The wall hangings were representations of Southern life, with riverboats, creeks, meadows, and mountains, and darkies a working in the fields. Everything was real elegant. Miss. Ball would have been real impressed.

"I hope ya'll are comfortable in here," said the servant. "If ya'll need anythin' in the night, jest pull on this here cord, an' I'll come up right quick. If ya'll can tell me when you want to get up, I'll make sure to wake ya'." I told him that we would like to get up with the sun, and he said he would see to it. As soon as our heads hit those goose down pillows, we were asleep. Sure enough, we were awakened at daylight by a servant telling us that "The Master wishes you to join him fer breakfast in the dinin' room in half an hour." So we did.

Breakfast, like supper the night before was served by the colored staff in the big dining room. I had never before seen such an amount of food set out for four people. Mrs. McKenna didn't eat breakfast, but wanted us to. There was hoecakes, toast, jam, bacon, ham, potatoes, eggs, sliced melon and fruit. There was also two kinds of gravy and sausage. Coffee was served with the meal. There was always a servant standing by Mr. McKenna, who directed the staff of servers.

Now, I'd never been served by anyone else before, and wasn't real sure how to act. I'd watched the night before, so I knew how to get what food I wanted without seeming like too much of a hayseed. I can tell you one thing, and that is that this surely made me appreciate the time Miss Ball spent trying to get me and Jack to mind our manners.

A plantation breakfast can last a long time, if you let it. Most folks I knew didn't have too much to say at mealtimes, but in polite company, you had to talk as you ate, and mind yer manners, too.

Mr. McKenna started telling us what was on his mind by saying, "Boys, yer on a grand adventure in more ways than you know, right now. Last night, Mrs. McKenna and I were discussin' ya'll, and allowed as how ya' were good boys, and wouldn't take old folks' advice amiss.

Ya'll are kind young fer what yer doin', but there really ain't no better time fer it. Ya' see boys, the South and time cain't wait 'til yer older to show you somethin'. The South ain't a place; it's a way of life. Southerners are a rare mixture of honor and an odd type of chivalry. King Arthur didn't have any braver knights, no, nor fairer ladies than are to be found in the South. Here, a man's word is his bond. Honor isn't just a word, but a concept that duels are fought for. Southerners have always been the first to fight for their beliefs. Why, ol' George Washington was a Southerner. So were Adams, Paine and Jefferson.

The South cain't be defeated, for it lives in men's minds and hearts. When young'uns are born to Southern parents, they'll be taught our values, and them that are born down in Mexico 'er out in California 'er even up in Idaho Territory will be as Southern as you an' me. So look around ya' boys, an' don't never fergit what ya' see, fer the world won't never see it's like again.

By each of yer plates," he continued, "you'll find a letter in an envelope. I've written each of ya' a letter of introduction to my factor in New Orleans, name of Nigel Reddington. He's a good man, even if he is English. He'll see that ya' have enough money to get home on if'n ya' run onto hard times. Mrs. McKenna don't want nothin' bad ta happen ta ya'll so call on ol' Nigel if'n ya' need him.

Boys, there's one more thing to tell ya'," he went on, "In a half day's ride, you'll come on the big river. Now, I know there ain't no use a warnin' ya', fer boys always wanna see an' do everything that even looks excitin'. Boys, be real careful, for in them dives on the waterfront, anywhere, for that matter, you'll find the toughest, hardest, cruelest, most wicked men in the world. Many of 'em will kill ya' for the change in yer pocket. Some of 'em will do it just 'cause they don't like yer looks.

Don't go gettin' into an argument 'er a fight with any of 'em if ya' don't have to. They'll gouge our yer eyes 'er stomp ya' to death. There ain't no such thing as a fair fight, an' if one of 'em thinks he's a losin', he'll pull a knife or a gun. He'll use a bottle or a club if he can get his hands on one, and he'll kill ya'.

Thing is, ya' don't have trouble with just one of 'em, neither. Ya' have ta fight 'em all. Worst part is, ya' cain't show no fear atall, 'er they'll be on ya' like stink on a polecat. If trouble even looks like it's about to develop, shoot first an' run like hell.

Keep in mind that most of 'em is riff raff and criminals, and there ain't no honor among 'em. Don't try ta deal with 'em on a gentleman's terms.

If yer in camp, don't all ya'll sleep at one time. Keep a guard posted and sleep with yer pistols under yer head even in a hotel room. If ya' hear an intruder, don't hesitate ta shoot, fer anybody a skulkin' around in the night sure ain't no friend a' yers.

Three young fellers like ya'll are sure ta look like easy pickin's fer yer horses 'er guns 'er what money ya' might have on ya'. So don't trust anyone 'cause it'll get ya' killed, sure."

After breakfast, which took a little too long to finish, Mr. and Mrs. McKenna saw us off. On the way down the drive, Thad remarked, "Ya' know, I could get real used ta bein' a planter an' havin' all a' them servants. Why someone even brushed my clothes an' hat whilst we slept."

The McKennas were still waving as we turned into the land and lost sight of them. They were real nice folks, and had asked us to stay with them again if we happened back that way. We were getting real excited about seeing the mighty Mississippi River, though, and we looked at each other, grinned, and gave a wild rebel yell and spurred for the river, the packhorses dragging behind.

Our first sight of the "Father of Waters," as the Indians called it, like to took our breath away. We had been told that in places it was a mile wide, but seeing it with our own eyes was a bunch different than seeing it in your mind. We sat there on our horses on a bluff overlooking a long stretch of the water, and couldn't get over how wide it really was. The largest river we'd seen was the Cumberland that we'd crossed just a few days earlier. Shoot, where we crossed, you could throw a rock across without trying too hard. Well, Sir, you ain't a fixing to throw a rock across this one, nor wade it on a horse, neither.

While we were watching, we got to see one of them riverboats we'd heard about a steaming upstream. She was white and looked like a fairy tale castle, what with all them decks and the gingerbread and such. Smoke was a boiling out of her stacks and she was a paddling to beat the band. We could hear music comin' from her, too. My, what a glorious sight she was. I hoped to get to ride on one just like her someday.

Most of the river between Memphis and Vicksburg was still in Confederate hands, but you were likely to run into a Yankee patrol most anyplace. We did run into a couple, but we were so young they didn't see much harm in letting us go on about our business. We lied something fierce to them Yanks. We told them our Pa was sending us someplace safe from the fighting that was a goin' on around our home.

We figured, rightly as it happened, that the Yanks would let us go on to New Orleans, for we knew that it had been in Yankee hands since last April. We learned from Mr. McKenna that some Yankee sailor named Farragut sailed forty six miles up the Mississippi, past the Confederate forts of Saint Phillip and Jackson, which were on opposite sides of the river. There had been a hard shelling from the forts, but Farragut lost only three ships and once past the forts engaged part of the

Confederate flotilla and defeated them. The next day, he took New Orleans and put ashore a Federal garrison.

The loss of New Orleans was a blow to the South, but most of the fighting was over east, anyhow. Over in Virginia, our friend J. E. B. Stuart rolled up Yankee general John Pope's right flank and helped Stonewall Jackson win a big battle just a few days ago, on August ninth. Ol' J. E. B. Stuart was on his way to making good his brag.

Loss to the South or not, we didn't care much that the Yanks held New Orleans. We wanted to see the sights, and New Orleans had always been said to be the finest and most exciting city in the South. There was bound to be fun to be had, and sights to see, and we weren't a fixin' to miss out on too much of it.

Well, we headed on downstream, watching sharp for any patrols. Either side would question us, and we didn't want to waste any more time on soldiers. Besides, wherever the armies were, there was bound to be deserters from both sides, out to rob and kill. Added to the river riff-raff Mr. McKenna had told us about made us a mite nervous 'bout meeting strangers.

The ride had been long and hard, and the horses needed rest as badly as we did. We found a place to camp across the river from where the Arkansas River dumps into the Mississippi, just outside Beulah. We camped away from the river, well above the highest waterline, for it was commencing to rain. I don't know if you've been in the deep south when it decided to rain, but I can tell you that it comes down in bucketsful. The rain is usually warm and the lightning jumps from high spot to high spot and makes flashes bright enough to read the paper by, if you were dumb enough to stand out in it and try. It's right scary the first few times you see it.

Now the whole area around where we stopped to camp was filled with caves, both shallow and deep. It wasn't no time to be exploring caves, so we picked us a shallow one, just big enough for us and the ponies and built a little fire. It was a good thing we found it, too, for it was too wet to pitch the tent, and with the lightning, you couldn't get under a tree.

Riding a hundred miles in two days, you can see how hard we pushed the animals. Wasn't too easy on us, neither. Would have been a sight easier if we'd been able to stay on the roads, but because of the Yanks, we were scared to.

Thad thought it would be a good place to rest up a couple of days, and me and Jack agreed. It was a good two days, too. Swimmin' in the river and takin' naps filled the day, and catfishin' took a good part of the night. We caught some beauties, too, and cooked them on a stick over the fire or rolled them in cornmeal and fried them in a pan.

I got in a lot of practice with my revolver, drawing and dry-firing. Now and then I'd shoot some powder and ball, just for fun. I could hit most anything within fifty or sixty feet by then, without aiming. It wouldn't have done any good to aim anyhow, for the gun had no front sight.

I hit my first moving target that first day. Jack and Thad were a watchin' me practice, like they always did. They thought it was right amusin', watching me work like that. They couldn't see any use in all that speed. They got a laugh out of watchin' me draw and aim about a hundred times without firing, and then watch' me fire a couple dozen rounds and cuss when I missed. They couldn't see any sense in it atall. Me, I was just hooked on it. I was in love with that pistol. Anyhow, I was practicing, and hadn't fired a shot yet.

I had just checked the loads and put the pistol back in the leather when a little ol' cottontail jumped up and started to run for it. I whipped out that six shooter and fired before I even had time to think about it. I fetched that gun so quick, Jack and

Thad didn't even see me draw. The bullet took the cottontail right in the neck and rolled him over a couple of times. I had aimed at the head, but had miscalculated his speed, and got him in the neck. I thought it was a fair shot even if he was only about forty feet away.

We used the cottontail for catfish bait and he worked pretty good. Me and Thad caught some average ones, but ol' Jack, he caught a ten pounder. A catfish steak and a little bit of salt, and you'd best not get between Thad and the trough. He'd run right over the top of you to get to eat some catfish.

CHAPTER FIVE

We started out at sunup the next day and rode along the river, not in any kind of a hurry and camped for the night near Greenville and the next night and the night after that. There weren't any towns near the river that we knew of, so we just roughed it in the woods. A lot of the way was pretty swampy, so the going was slow. We had to watch for snakes a lot, it being so swampy and all, cottonmouths and copperheads were thicker n' hair on a dog's back. We pushed pretty hard, but had to cross a river and got everything we owned wet, so we made camp about half a day's ride north of Vicksburg, Mississippi.

Vicksburg was still in Confederate hands, and thought to be one of the best fortified places in the south, so that's where we were trying to go when we got everything wet. We wanted to be dry and clean when we got to town, so we unpacked everything to dry. After making camp, the first thing we did was clean, oil and reload all the guns. Then we cooked some supper and sat around on logs waitin' for our bedding to get dry enough to sleep in. Good thing for us it was late August, so we weren't a bit cold, just uncomfortable.

As we sat around talking, getting ready for bed, I had a thought. "Boys," I asked, "you know how we wanted to ride one of them big river boats? Well, how 'bout we leave the horses and all our gear in Vicksburg, and just take our clothes and sidearms and get on one of them boats and ride her clear into New Orleans, or at least to Baton Rouge, and then we'll figure some way to get through the Federal lines to New Orleans."

"Sounds good to me," Thad agreed. "Vicksburg is a good place to leave our gear. It won't get stole by no Yankees there."

"Besides," throws in Jack, "our story about Pa sending us to New Orleans will hold water better if we seem like normal kids."

So that's what we decided to do. It wasn't but a few minutes 'til Thad and I were fast asleep, and Jack hiding in the shadows, to watch. It was about midnight when I awakened in a panic by a hand over my mouth. As soon as I was awake, Jack whispers in my ear, "I think someone's out there." I nodded my head and he turned loose of my mouth.

I put my mouth real close to his ear and said, "Wake Thad whilst I get my gun belt on. You two stay in the shadows with your rifles. I'll see what's goin' on."

My heart was pounding like a trip hammer, and it was hard for me to breathe. I just calmly walked over to the campfire, which had burned down real low, and threw some more wood on it. Then I reached down and poured a cup of coffee from the pot and stood near the fire drinking coffee with the cup in my left hand. I was surprised that my hand didn't shake so to spill the coffee. I just stood there like I hadn't a care in the world, and didn't know I was being watched. There was quite a lot of light from the fire now, so I stepped back from it a few feet. All I had to do now was wait. I touched Ma's Testament, in my shirt pocket, for luck.

I waited about two minutes before I heard a twig snap in the brush and beyond the firelight, and a gravelly voice said, "Don't move, Bub." and two men stepped into the firelight directly across from me.

One of them was a huge man, well over six feet tall and heavy, without being fat, and looked like a bear with his full black beard. He even had a black mat of hair showin' at his throat, above his second shirt button. If the first man looked like a bear, the second one looked like a weasel. He had a pointed face and quick, furtive movements, skinny and had a scraggely beard. Just about then I heard a rustling in the brush behind me, and a sharp cry. Two other men came into the light, pushin' Jack before them.

"We found this'n here watchin' the camp with this here carbine. Had to warp him one 'long side the head."

Sure enough, Jack was bleeding over his right ear. Looked like one of them hit Jack with a pistol barrel. Bear and Weasel held their guns on us while one of them took a look at Jack to make sure he didn't have a pistol on him. They'd already taken his carbine. They noticed his belt knife, and took it, too.

"Give over yer knife an' pistol, boy, an' we might let ya'll walk outta here alive," said the Bear to me. Just then Jack started to cry. Them fellers didn't know it yet, but when ol' Jack got so mad or scared he started to cry, you best crawl in a hole an' pull the hole in after ya', for Jack goes plumb crazy. He reached up to touch his head where it was bleeding, and I knew what he was a gonna do next.

Jack drew an' threw that knife he carried in the neck of his shirt and it took one of the men that had brought him in right in the middle of the chest. I drew that pistol I was so in love with, and shot Weasel in the stomach, drew a little right and shot Bear twice in the chest, and turned back and shot Weasel once more. There was a lot of gunfire a goin' on and I all of a sudden found myself flat on my back and didn't know how I got there. A carbine boomed, and I knew ol' Thad had got in on it, too.

I was so scairt that I like to wet my pants. My whole upper body was a throbbin' and it came to me that I'd been shot again. I was a havin' trouble breathin', so I was sure that this time I was a gonna die. I could feel warm blood a runnin' down under my arm, so I put my hand over the hurt place and felt Ma's Testament. I figured that I was gonna be joining her soon, so it was right comfortin' to me to feel that little Bible. Ma had given it to me when I was real little, and when we left home, I had started to carry it in my shirt pocket. I didn't want them other two to know it, though, for they'd a' teased me terrible, an' called me "Preacher." It was a comfort to me now, though.

Thad stepped into the firelight, then, and his face was ashen. Jack was curled up in a little ball and was a moanin'. Thad leaned over Jack to check the damage first, then walked over to where I lay, and knelt down beside me. The front of my shirt was bloody, and when Thad drew his bloody hand away from me, I threw up. When I vomited, Thad did, too. He always did have a weak stomach.

I whispered, "Thad, gimme Ma's Testament outta my shirt pocket, fer I wanna hold it whilst I croak."

Thad fumbled the Testament out of my bloody shirt and put it into my hand. Then he ripped open my shirt and looked at the wound. He prodded the wound with his finger and said, "Durned if'n there ain't a lump under yer hide. I cain't believe it, but I think that lump's the ball." I craned my neck to look at the wound, and watched as Thad squeezed that flattened ball outta my chest like a big pimple.

It hurt something fierce whilst he was a probin' around like that, but he kept on at it. "Yer durn lucky," Thad murmured. "Ya' got a couple of broke ribs, but the hole ain't too deep. I reckon yer a gonna live a while yet." Thad bandaged up my whole chest, so's to stop the bleeding. I had been a clutchin' Ma's Testament so hard my hand ached.

When I relaxed a little, I noticed the little Bible felt kinda funny, so I raised it up to take a look at it. That dratted pistol ball had hit that Testament dead center and gone all the way through, from Matthew through Revelation and out the back. Cowhide cover an' all. It was like Ma had reached down from heaven to take care of me still.

After a little while, I got up and moved over to sit with Jack and Thad. We just sat there a lookin' at what used to be four men. My chest was a achin' bad, and startin' to turn real black an' blue.

Thad said, "Jack, boy, I reckon you might could have a 'cussion in yer haid."

"I ain't got no 'cussion, ya' durn fool, what I got is a bad headache," Jack retorted.

"A lookin' at them fellers kindly makes me weak n' trembly in my innards," Thad opined.

Jack said, "Them sonsabitches had it comin'. I wisht that'n there was still alive so we could kill 'im again. My head is swolled up like a poisoned pup, an' hurts like sin."

Jack was a tough little devil, an' kinda like a bumblebee, you had to kill him or just leave him alone.

We sat there by the fire trying to figure out what to do. Thad was for breaking camp and high tailing it outta there. Jack didn't care what we did. In the end, we decided to play real cagey. Thad and I volunteered to look for the dead men's mounts if Jack would go through their pockets to see if we could find out anything about them. I would a' done it, but my left arm wouldn't work too good right then.

Jack said he would, so me and Thad started to circle camp in opposite directions. After ten minutes or so, I heard Thad whistle and made my way back to camp. Thad had heard the horses snort in the dark, and found them tied in the brush. He brought them into camp.

We unsaddled their horses and went through the saddlebags. Thad found over twenty-two hundred in Yankee money, and near five hundred in Confederate bills. Jack had found about two hundred fifty in gold and a few bills in their pockets. None of the dead men had anything to identify them in their possessions. We took three of the men to be deserters from the Union Army because of the remnants of uniforms they wore. I don't know about the fourth one.

I never thought much about dead folks before. It was eerie sitting by the fire looking at them dead bodies, knowing I made them dead. I guess I thought that when folks got shot they just kind of fell over and lay still. T'aint so. When I shot the weasel, he screamed somethin' fierce, and rolled up in a ball. He hollered "Oh, God, Oh, God!" and when I shot him the second time, he jerked real bad and kicked his feet on the ground.

Bear, on the other hand, flopped around like a chicken does when you chop off his head and made terrible noises. The one Jack knifed screamed and hollered for his Mama and clawed at the knife stuck in his heart 'til he died. Even after they laid there for a minute, they would twitch, sometimes.

By the time we got the horses back to camp, you could sometimes hear one of them pass gas. They had fouled themselves, too. We just sat there, looking at them, wondering what to do with the bodies. The only one that just dropped and laid still was the one Thad shot in the head. Thad looked a little green around the gills, yet, and I felt downright bad. It didn't seem to bother Jack atall. 'Course he had been whopped 'long side the head, and had a powerful mad on.

We decided to drag the dead men off the brush a ways and cover them up with some leaves and bushes. We didn't have anything to dig a proper grave with, and didn't want them right there in camp. We figured to let their horses go in the morning, as we rode out so they wouldn't go home tonight and make people wonder where their riders were. They didn't have anything we wanted except the money and food in their saddlebags. We didn't want their guns or knives, neither.

Sleep was out of the question, so we made some coffee and sat there talkin' and waitin' for mornin' to come. Thad said, "Tag, I seen how fast you fetched out that pistol. How's about you help me cut down my holster, like you done. I reckon I'll practice with you ever' mornin'."

Jack chimed in with, "Yep, me, too." So we spent the next little while cutting leather. I didn't guess they would laugh at me no more.

"You reckon them fellers' ghosts is hangin' 'round here, Tag?" asked Thad.

"Don't be a fool, Thad," pipes up Jack, "they ain't no such thing as ghosts, is there, Tag?"

"I don't rightly know," says I. "Reckon there are ghosts, or spirits or souls and such, 'cause ol' man Smith, the preacher at home, says everyone has a soul. Ol' Mammy Jewel, down at Mr. Porter's place, says there's ghosts all over, of folks that have been kilt. Why, Injuns even believe in ghosts and spirits. They's even a Holy Spirit."

"Well," said Thad, "I don't feel real comfortable, thinkin' of them folks' ghosts hangin' round watchin' us. Makes the hair kinder stand up on the back of my neck."

"Will you cut it out, 'bout them ghosts!" Jack says. "I ain't ascared of no ghost. They cain't hurt ya' nohow, can they Tag?"

"Well, I ain't no ghost expert, but I reckon yer right as rain, Jack. 'Nuff talkin' 'bout ghosts."

"Well, if we cain't talk 'bout ghosts," says Thad, "you reckon them men went to heaven or hell?"

"Thad, you horse's butt," says Jack, "Jesus ain't a fixin' to let them sonsabitches inta heaven. I don't want those sonsabitches a flappin' their wings 'round where my Ma is at, do you, Tag?"

"Well, come to think on it, no, I don't," I says. "Besides, that bearish one looked like a devil, sure 'nuff."

"Well, then," says Thad, "what about that weasely lookin' one that was a hollerin' 'Jesus, Jesus!' You 'spose he got in?"

"He weren't hollerin' 'Jesus, Jesus.' He was hollerin' 'Oh, God, Oh, God,'" Jack threw in. "It don't make no difference, nohow. Why you so concerned where them fellers went, anyhow?"

"I ain't never kilt no one before, and it kinder gets to me that I may of sent someone to hell," says Thad.

I didn't want to talk about it no more, so I said, "We didn't have no choice. They would have done us in, for sure. We did the killin', but we got to let the Lord sort out the souls. We cain't do nothin' 'bout that." I was real tired of this line of talk. I felt bad enough, anyhow. Talkin' 'bout souls and hell and such sure ain't my idea of a restful conversation. It just gets a body agitated.

It was starting to get light over in the east, so we got ready to go, and packed up all of our gear and saddled the horses. Jack had found a couple of opened bottles of whiskey in the dead men's saddlebags, so we ripped up some of their long johns and made him a new bandage. We soaked the bandage in whiskey and washed out the gash in Jack's head. Boy, did he squawk when that ol' whiskey hit the cut! I wanted to practice with my gun, but we figured we'd ride on for a couple of hours first, so no one would get curious about gunfire and find them bodies too soon. We stopped about half way to Vicksburg and spent about an hour practicing. Thad and Jack joined in this time.

We dodged around a couple of military patrols that morning. We didn't know if they were ours or Federals, so we just kept out of sight. We could hear them, but we never did see them. As we approached Vicksburg, we had to pass some sentries. We told them our story, and they passed us through. I guess we didn't look much like Yankee spies.

Vicksburg was one of the most heavily defended cities in the South. Earthworks were thrown up, and the bluffs were lined with cannon. Soldiers were everywhere. There was an abundance of supplies, and life was still good there. Vicksburg itself and the whole vicinity was covered with caves, and a lot of these had been made into some kind of shelter, in case the Yankees tried to take the town.

Vicksburg was right on the river, and a real necessity to the South for a couple of reasons. One was to allow Southern control of the river for trade and re-supply, but more important was to keep the Yankees from controlling the whole Mississippi. As long as Vicksburg was in Confederate hands, the Yankees could not use the river to transport troops, and must maintain two armies to try to control the countryside.

We put the horses in a stable, and told the owner that we might leave them with him for several weeks, and paid him a deposit. One half in Confederate money and one half in gold. We told him that if the worst happened and the Yanks took Vicksburg, that he should shoot the horses before letting them fall into Yankee hands, and he said, "That ain't likely, 'cause the South ain't never goin' to give up Vicksburg, but I'll shoot the 'harses' first."

I didn't know then how Vicksburg was going to figure in my future. There was a lot of patriotic fervor in Vicksburg. Spirits were high, and people didn't seem to care that down river was all in Federal hands. They seemed to believe Vicksburg was representative of the whole South, figuring that with most of the fighting in the east, the Yankees were only along the Mississippi temporarily. They thought Lee would be along before too long to rout out the damn Yankees and send them back up north with their tails between their legs.

After all, hadn't the Confederate Army been victorious almost all the time, in almost every engagement? So what, if the Federals held most of the river. It didn't matter that the Union had the strongest Navy, this was a land war. Didn't the South have control of most of the southeast? Wasn't Washington, D.C. in danger? Even ol' Lincoln was afraid to leave the Capitol, and held the whole Army of the Potomac around him, he was so afraid. What really made the Southern gentry mad enough to jump up and down, was that back in June, ol' Abe had said that the "Rebel" States had until January 1, 1863 to lay down their arms and re-join the Union, or he was going to free their slaves by a Proclamation of Emancipation. The stableman said, "Why, that Lincoln cain't even win a battle. How in tarnation does he think he can take our servants and free 'em? An' what about States like Kentucky and Maryland that stayed in the Union. Folks there had slaves; were they to go free or not? Ol' Abe ain't thought that out too well, atall."

Well, I hope it ain't so, but ol' Mr. McKenna might be right after all. We walked down the street, and got a room at a cheap hotel, then hunted up an eating house to have an early dinner. After not getting any sleep the night before, we decided to turn in early and get some rest before going sightseeing. We really had to fight ourselves, though, for young men just naturally want to do everything right this minute. We went to a general store, first and bought some more powder and ball. We wouldn't have our carbines for a while, so we got a lot of ball for our pistols, which we decided to wear under our vests, in our belts instead of out where folks could see them. We figured this would make our story about being sent away from the fighting seem more believable to the folks we happened to meet.

We awoke the next mornin' to the sound of a city coming to life. Vicksburg was the biggest city around, and was the center of commerce for this area, and woke up pretty early. We were excited to get on out and see what was a going on. We had breakfast in an eating house a couple of doors down from the hotel, and went out to see what we could see.

Jack bought some more candy, and was already eating it this early in the day. I have to admit that I ate some of it, too. Vicksburg was an exciting place. Lots of soldiers had time off and were already getting rowdy in the taverns, and townsfolks were keepin' up with them in takin' their money. The stores had more of everything than any we had ever been in before. We talked to everybody that had time to talk to kids. We found out that we were staying in the seedier part of town, for there were fine homes on the other side. Why, some of them were as fine as any of the mansions on the plantations. Makes you wonder what them folks did for a living.

Lots of black folks were sweeping walks and streets and hauling wood and doing laundry and such. I'd never seen so much activity. They had big churches and schools and everything, while over by where we were staying, they had shanties and no yards. Some of those folks were dirt poor. Boats came in ever so often loaded with wood and coal, for it was near the first week in September, and though it wasn't too cold yet, fall was comin' on, and with it the rains.

We spent three days in Vicksburg just lounging around and lookin' at things. Seeing how other people lived was a real revelation. We had thought that everyone was just like us. After meeting some of the planters on our trip, and seein' how city folks lived, we felt kind of deprived, coming' from the back woods and all. It seemed real strange to us when talkin' to some of the city kids to find out that they thought that we were the lucky ones. They were jealous because we had so much more freedom than they did. We had left home to see the world. We had horses and things, and lived where people let us alone to shift for ourselves, smoke, go fishin' and huntin' and scratch our behinds and spit when we had a mind to. I guess that's when I learned that everyone thinks the other guy has a better deal in life.

Though the Yankees controlled most of the river, folks were sneakin' in and out of the city to go other places most every night. We had thought to get a ride on one of them river boats that looked like floatin' palaces, but they weren't comin' to Vicksburg any more on account of the Yankees. That being the case, we made a deal with a man and his black, whom we had met in the wood yard, to catch a ride south after dark. He told us that he was just going to drift with the current down to Alcorn, but that we might be able to get another boat from there, to go on down to Natchez.

We left with them that night, and paddled out into the middle of the river, so as not to be seen by Federal patrols, and just drifted with the current. All we had with us was our saddlebags and bedrolls, so we didn't take up too much room. This was a small boat, maybe eighteen feet long that had been built in Vicksburg for just such a purpose as this. Milo, the white man, said that each time he slipped into Vicksburg with another load of goods to sell, he bought another boat, or sometimes a raft to drift on home in. He said that when he got home, he would sell the boat or the logs from the raft and do it all over again on the next trip. It took us two nights, drifting, to get to Alcorn, for we laid up days on some island in the middle of the river so as to keep away from the Yankees.

We spent a day at Milo's home and made a deal with a bunch of woodcutters about our ages to get a ride with them on down to Natchez on a big raft of logs they intended to sell there. They said it was a right good living, selling logs to city folks for building and firewood and such. It looked to be a right good life, too, for them boys was free as birds. They would build a little cabin on the raft to cook in or get out of the rain in, and just drift along, smokin', fishin' and sleeping.

They told us it wasn't so easy cutting the logs and haulin' them to the river to build the rafts, but that it was worth it for the river trip. They had been as far south as New Orleans, so we asked a lot of questions, and they sure did fill our ears. I 'spect that they were a lyin' some, but it sure made a good story, lies or not.

We traveled in the daytime as well as evening on the raft, but not at night, for the boys told us that they had got hung up on sandbars before and had to take the raft apart to get it free. In the three days it took us to float to Natchez, we got stopped by Yankees twice, but they let us go, we were so young lookin'.

We got into Natchez easy as pie, riding that raft, and wandered away from the waterfront looking for a hotel to put up in. We finally found one not too many blocks away, stowed our gear and set out to find something to eat.

Now, Natchez in them days was known far and wide for its seamier side. Parts, even most, of the town was respectable, but the part we stayed in was a real hot spot. You'd think that sooner or later we'd learn to look a place over before lightin' somewhere, but being hillbillies, we didn't know any better. Natchez Under the River, as the waterfront was known was reputed to be the harbor for the most notorious thieves, gamblers, cut throats, muggers, murderers and sinners in the South. I believed it, too, for everywhere you looked you could see someone you'd rather not turn your back on. There were lots of taverns and other dives that ran full tilt all day and all night, but the later the hour, the greater the chance that you would lose your money or your life.

Before the war, there had been a good sized slave market here, but nowadays, it was deserted. No one was buying servants these days. The place was just a bustle with folks a coming and going. Because of the Yankee presence, life was going at a fast pace as if by frenzied activity, the people could stave off the effects of the war.

Prices of goods were higher here than anyplace we'd seen yet. All the merchants were charging more for they didn't know when the next shipment of goods would arrive, and they wanted all the money they could get. It was sad that Confederate money was being discounted as much as fifty per cent in some places.

We wanted to hustle up some excitement, naturally, so we decided to slip into a tavern acting grown up. We walked into the Alhambra and found a table in a corner, near the door, where we could all sit with our backs to the wall. I sat in the middle with Thad on one side of me and Jack on the other, and we felt pretty secure that way. There was lots of smoke in the air and the music was loud. Thad went up to the bar and ordered the beer, so we sat watchin' all the activity and drinkin'. Girls were workin' the customers to a fare thee well, and as we watched, there must have been three or four fistfights break out over nothin' at all. Just high spirits, I reckon. There was loud laughter and cussin' and a general feeling' of wildness in there.

We had a couple of beers each and were starting to feel a mite dizzy, so I suggested that we take a walk outside for some fresh air before we had any more to drink. Now, Jack, he could think up more devilment than Thad and me together, and we were no more than outside in the night air until he had this idea. It was his idea to shinny up the porch poles of the building next door and get on the roof so's we could peek in the upstairs windows to the tavern and see, maybe, what them two dollar favors really was.

With our bellies full of beer, it seemed like a right good idea, so we stacked some barrels and boxes up and climbed the posts 'til we got up on the roof. It was kind of rickety, so we had to be real careful just where we stepped. The building we were on was only one story, so we could lay on the opposite side of the roof and look over the ridgeline and see into some of the upstairs rooms.

Jack made it to the ridge first, looked over and whispered, "Good God A' Mighty. Hurry up, fellers, ya' ain't gonna b'lieve yer eyes!"

Thad and I hurried on up and threw ourselves down beside Jack and learned that he was right. We couldn't believe our eyes. Why, our eyes bugged out 'til we looked like three stomped on frogs, for in that room stood the first nekkid lady we ever seen. Well, she wasn't quite nekkid when we first seen her, but she sure was a gettin' that way. She had dark, curly hair, painted lips and big, blue eyes. I thought she was the most beautiful creature I had ever seen. Jack and Thad thought so, too.

Well, then this gent we hadn't noticed before stepped over and gave her some bills, then stepped back some. She laughed and waved the money at him playfully, and she went over to push them bills into a little slot in the wall, and turned to face the man. She put her thumbs into the clothes at her waist, and bending, pushed them to the floor. When she stood up again, all she was wearin' was a big smile, stockings that looked like they were made of fishing net and some little red shoes. Well, we're kinda slow, but I reckon we figured out what them two dollar favors was.

We stayed in Natchez about another week, and finally met up with a kid 'bout our own age, name a' Tom. He seemed like a nice enough feller. Tom was kinder different from us, though, for he had carroty colored hair an' freckles on all the skin I could see. Skinny, with bright blue eyes, he seemed like an innocent to us. Ol' Tom was a takin' a skiff on down to New Orleans, where his Ma and he lived, and offered us a ride if we'd take our turns at the oars. There was so many Yanks down thataway, we was going to hole up on some islands at night. Me an' Jack an' Thad decided that we'd winter in New Orleans, if we could, even if it was in Yankee hands. We didn't figger 'em to pay no mind to a bunch a' kids.

It took the better part of three days to get on down there, a driftin' along like we were. It was a good time for us, a' lazing along and talkin' and a' fishin'. Caught some nice ones, too, and cooked them when we stopped on the islands for the night.

Tom said there weren't no snakes on them islands, but we had to watch for crooks, runaway slaves and the durned Yankees, who we considered worst of all.

Twice, we saw military horses washed up dead, with their gear still on, and once saw a dead man. He was a soldier, according to his clothes, but he was so swole up and odiferous that we didn't get close enough to see what side he was on. We hoped he was a Yank, though.

We stayed 'bout three days in Baton Rouge, just a loafin' and then left for New Orleans, Queen of the South.

CHAPTER SIX

We just floated along and weren't in any hurry, because we wanted to slip into New Orleans under the cover of dark, and sneak around the Yankees. Tom said it wasn't too hard for a kid to do, so we were going to let him lead the way.

Tom said, "Them Yankees is pretty dumb, why there are lots of places to sneak in and out and not get caught. We might have to hide some in a cemetery, but ya'll ain't a scared of ghosts, are ya'?"

"Hell, no!" said Jack. "We don't pay 'em no mind. We don't mess with them, so they don't mess with us. 'Sides, we never done 'em no harm whilst they was a livin' so they hadn't oughta be mad at us, nohow."

Tom said that since the Yankees had occupied the city in April, they had put it under martial law and everyone had to be off the streets by ten o'clock at night because of the curfew. He said that the Yanks would cart you right off to a military jail for who knows how long, so when we got in the city, we slipped from one shadow to another and from bush to bush and only had to outwait two Yankee patrols before getting to Tom's place.

Tom said he didn't have a Dad, but lived with his Ma and aunt. They had rented the coach house of one of the shabbier mansions down near the lower part of town, not far from where the rougher neighborhoods started. The folks who owned the big house only lived in part of it, and had lost their fortune due to the wastrel son who was shot in a duel in '59. They rented rooms in the big house and some of the out buildings to some of the poorer folk, and got just enough to live on in rents. Tom's Ma taught school, and his aunt took in ironing and washed clothes for the troops. First the Confederates, and after the occupation, the Federals.

When we sneaked in the yard and tapped on the door, Tom's Ma opened it and dragged ol' Tom inside by the ear. Then she saw us and drew us inside too, before sayin' a word.

"Where have you been for nearly two weeks?" she asked with a fierce scowl. "Tom, Tom, whatever am I going to do with you?" Tears were starting to roll down her cheeks. "I've been worried sick. We've looked all over for you. We've even gone to the Yankees to try to get them to look for you. Who are your ragamuffin friends?"

"Ma, slow down. I'm alright and these here boys are tryin' ta get away from the fightin'. Their Pa was worried they might get hurt. Ma, you shouldn't oughta gone to the Yanks. Now I'll be marked by them as a troublemaker."

Seems there was a little more to Tom than he had told us. He had overheard his Ma and his aunt talkin' about not havin' enough money, and worrying how they were going to survive, and ol' Tom decided to do somethin' about it. When he got his Ma calmed down a little, he gave her a leather poke with some money in it. I don't know how much, and he didn't say, but it was quite a little. Seems that Tom and his friend had stolen a bunch of booze and medical supplies from an unwatched Yankee supply wagon, loaded them in that skiff and traveled north, only moving at night, same as we did coming in here. They had sold those supplies up river and Tom's friend had stayed in Natchez. Tom had come home with his share of the money and given it to his Ma. After showing us where we would sleep, she went to bed and left us alone to talk for a while before turning in.

Tom said we should walk around town during the daytime, so we'd know the layout before night fall, so we wouldn't have any trouble coming home. It sounded like a good idea to us, so we did just that. We had thought, at first, that we would spend the winter in New Orleans, but after the first day, seeing how the Yankees treated the people, and what a powder keg the city was turning into, we decided that we'd find somewhere else warm to winter. We wanted to get our fill of New Orleans, first, though. Boy, did we ever. New Orleans was known far and wide for its sinful ways and general wickedness.

The city was far bigger than anyplace we'd seen before, and Thad remarked, "D'ya'll ever kick an ant hill and watch them rascals scurry and scuttle 'round? Well, this whole durn place looks to be a red ant hill ta me. Looks to be a pretty good place to get stung, ya' ain't keerful. They's places I ain't about to go after dark. Looks bad enough in the day time."

As night fell, we were surprised that the activity didn't seem to slow. Tom said people used to keep going all night, but the Yankees were awful concerned about rebellion and spies. Tom said that if we wanted to see some of the hot spots, we best get her done, so we could be off the streets before curfew.

Thad and Jack and I had become sort of used to comin' and goin' as we pleased, and that Yankee curfew just wasn't much fun. On a normal day, we'd think ten o'clock was pretty late. Matter of fact, we'd probably have been in bed by that time at home.

After a week or so of coming in before ten o'clock, we decided to do a little scoutin' around after curfew to see what the damnyankees were a doin'. Damnyankee is one word in the South. Was then and still is, most places. Anyway, we would come home about nine-thirty and talk awhile, and make like we were goin' to bed, so as not to worry Tom's Ma. So far, we'd been pretty good, only we figured that if the Yankees wanted everyone off the streets so early, there must be somethin' goin' on.

Now, young boys have been sneakin' out of houses as long as people have been building them. I expect that cave boys snuck out too. I reckon that even Indians out west sneaked out. There is something real powerful that draws boys out at night. Why, just thinkin' there might be something to see or do out there in the dark just works on a boy 'til he don't have a choice.

We were kind of cautious about where we went when we snuck out, though. We figured if we got caught by Yankees, we'd likely get turned loose after a hiding or something, because of our ages. We figured if we acted a little sissy, and maybe even cried some, the Yanks would send us home, or at the worse escort us. One way or another, we just had to see the city after dark.

We were real surprised to see how many folks were out and about when there was supposed to be a curfew in force. We didn't know about passes and such, nor about the number of people a working for the Yanks, neither. Artisans, feed suppliers, merchants selling produce and washer women, why, you just wouldn't expect to see a whole 'nother city come to life after curfew.

Another thing we noticed, seeing as how we were a slippin' around in the dark ourselves, was that every so often, we would see other furtive shadows flit from dark place to dark place.

Tom said, "They's a whole lot a' folks a goin' out at night ta do the Yankees dirt. They crack wagon spokes, lame animals, and cut rigging, put gravel in the beans and do as much devilment as they can without gettin' caught. Why they's some folks that even kill lone Yanks so's they're ascared ta go out at night, 'less they go in a bunch.

Other folks," he went on, "just steal the stuff to sell to Southerners on the black market. If they get caught doin' them things, the Yanks'll hang 'em sure."

There were lots of free black folks in New Orleans, even before the Yankees came. So many, in fact, that they had their own section of the city, called "The Quarter." Now, I don't know if it was a quarter of the city or not, but it was pretty big. Many of them had their own shops, and homes. All the trades were there, from heathen voodoo people to undertakers. From green grocers to furniture makers. Wheelwrights, coopers, blacksmiths, why, the colored folks had their own city right there among the whites. Educated people. They even had their own system. Some of them owned their own slaves, and some of them were so anti-slave that they wouldn't own one, but paid wages to other free black folks.

We began to see that the Federals had an abundance of everything. Horses, equipment, uniforms, food, wagons, cannons, lots and lots of supplies. We also began to see that the people of New Orleans were starting to feel the pinch of war. Everyone that didn't cooperate or cater to the Federals was having a hard time, while those that did, were getting some luxuries. This got to botherin' us awful bad.

We looked up Mr. McKenna's agent, Nigel Reddington, one morning, and found that English and other foreign firms were doing a bang up business with the Federals. We had to wait in the lobby 'til a girl took our letters in to him and came back to get us. I didn't know you had to make an 'appointment with a secretary' just to get to see a feller. I guess important folks are too busy to see some kids. I guess important folks are too busy to see just anybody. The letters got his attention, though.

Reddington himself came out to get us and took us into his office. He said, "Mr. McKenna is an old and valued client. He's also my friend. I'll help you anyway I can, so if you need me for anything, just let me know. Is there anything I can do for you now, or is this a social visit?"

"Well," I says, "I'm right glad to meet you, too, Mr. Reddington. We do have something you might help us with. Ya' see, we have a pretty good pile a' money, and we are afraid of gettin' robbed or losin' it. Mr. McKenna said you could take it off our hands and put it to work somewheres and we'd sure be beholden."

"Why, I'd be happy to invest it for you. I will have to discount Confederate money by thirty-five percentum, though. I hope you understand," said Reddington.

"We ain't got too much Confederate money, Sir," I say. "We got mostly Federal dollars. We want to put seven thousand Yankee dollars with you and enough Confederate and gold to make up another five hundred, so we'll each have twenty-five hundred."

Well sir, that got his attention again. He said, "That's a considerable sum for three young men. I can promise you that your investment will be secure. Let me have Sarah open a draw account for each of you.

I want you to understand that the earnings from your money will be deposited in a bank at Liverpool, England, where Mr. McKenna has his funds. You would, of course, have a draw account equal to ten percent of the total at any given time, right through this office. After the first six months, you can cash out at anytime, in gold, here in New Orleans or in any major city where we have an office. We will make each of you beneficiaries of the others' trust in the event something should happen to one of you. Will that be satisfactory?"

"Why, sure," says we. Shoot, we didn't know what he was talkin' about, anyway. All we knew was that them Yankee dollars were out of our hands, because they wasn't any good to us, now, anyhow.

We kept enough money to play with, but we were becoming aware just how much we had already spent and decided to look around for some more. We had heard that both armies needed beef something fierce. I remembered that Pa had said that when he was in Texas and Mexico, he saw them Spanish cattle runnin' wild all over. He said that they were descended from cattle that had escaped from the old Spaniards that had explored the whole Southwest, two hundred years before.

The only cattle we had any experience with were the cows at home. We had herded a couple of dozen at a time once or twice, but not in the amount that we were talkin' about here. We figured to hire on with some rancher 'til we learned the ropes, or to hire someone who did. We knew we would have the devil's own job just trying to get wild cattle out of the brush, let alone herd them for any distance. We knew how a cow acts when it's sick, and we knew about cutting bull calves, after all, we did live on a farm so weren't completely dumb; we just acted like it sometimes.

We were surely a havin' fun sneakin' around New Orleans, anyhow. It seems like it's always more fun when you're doin' somethin' you're not supposed to do, ain't it? Anyhow, after sneakin' out for a few nights, we began to notice a pattern in the guard routine. We didn't want to get caught out after curfew, so we paid close attention to such details. We saw that if we really wanted to, we could sneak right into the warehouses and see what they had stored in there. The guards were more interested in playin' cards than they were in guardin' everything. They were interested in the ladies of the evening that hung around wherever there were troops. You know that there has always been camp followers. They followed the Roman Legions, and Attila the Hun, and they still follow the troops today. The faces and races change, but the camp followers won't never change.

We noticed the backs of the warehouses weren't hardly guarded atall, and only now and then would a trooper go around back to take a look, so we figured we could come up with a way to get in and out again without gettin' caught.

We made a plan that seemed foolproof and said that sometime we just might do it. Just a walkin' 'round in New Orleans was an adventure. Part of its spice came from the idea that we weren't supposed to be out, but part of it was the sheer joy of bein' young and seein' the sights and smellin' the smells. Everywhere you turned was a new scent. You could smell the flowers, and the food being cooked, and when you walked by a shop, you could tell what was sold inside without using your eyes. Tobacco, spices, furniture wax, leather, hemp, food, chemicals, fish and everything else under the sun, and underlying all the other scents, horse dung. Even though there were street sweepers, the odor of decaying fruit and dishwater and horse dung pervaded the night. Part of the smell was made up of unwashed human bodies, too. Like I said, everything under the sun. It was amazing and wonderful world to four young men.

On the night we finally worked up our nerve to sneak into one of the warehouses, it was overcast, and without the light from some of the oil street lights, it was blacker than the inside of a cow. The troops always had lanterns at the guard posts, and many of the walking patrols carried them, too. We had chosen the largest of the warehouses and had waited until two o'clock in the morning to go out, figuring the guards would be tired and not as alert as they should be.

The warehouses were all next to each other, down by the river. Most of them were just one story high, and had double doors front and rear, so a team and wagon could drive in one end and out the other, turning into an alley. Most of them didn't have windows, either, which was real handy for what we wanted to do.

Each of us had a candle about three inches long. This would be a quick look at what was in this building, so we wouldn't need light for very long. Tom had come up with some of the new Lucifer match sticks that would strike anywhere, so we were all set. We left our weapons back at Tom's house, hid real well. We figured that if the Yanks caught us, we would probably not get punished too bad if they thought we were just mischief makers, and not armed robbers.

It was pitch black and starting to rain when we got into position. The rain made the guards want to keep dry, so they stayed under an awning in front, and for the hour we watched them, they only took a look out back once, so we sneaked a look at the back door, and saw that it was like a big barn door, and that countless wagons had made a groove about six inches deep under the door, and that the wood was rotted and eaten by termites and such 'til we could break away enough to make a hole to squeeze through, if we slithered on our backs.

Well, we wriggled under there one at a time, trying not to make any noise, and once inside just stood there awhile listening. Warehouses and storerooms and cellars have a smell of their very own. Burlap, leather, oil, dust and such. They usually smell dry and musty.

Now, this was a pretty tight built building, and if we kept away from the doors, we were pretty safe in that the candle light probably wouldn't be seen by the guards. We lit our candles, and by waving our arms a lot and mouthing words so as not to whisper or make any noises, we got across to each other just what we were going to do. We should have planned it out a little better, but a feller just can't think of everything at once, never havin' been a burglar before.

We split up and started pokin' around. The Federals had all kinds of stuff in there, and I found case after case of them new 'airtights.' You know what I mean, them tin tubes that they heat and solder shut so that the food won't spoil so fast. They had beef and tomatoes and other vegetables in them tins. Mostly food and such in my corner. My candle had burned almost down, so we met back at the door and got ready to leave. Thad laid down and started to crawl under the door, and froze, halfway out. He waited five minutes, then went on out. I followed then Tom and then Jack.

After we were safely away, I asked, "Thad, how come you waited so long in that hole?"

"Well, durn it," he answered, "one of them Yanks decided that the side of the building would make a good out house. He durn near hit me in the face. I did get splashed a little, and it sure was hard ta hold still. Next time, one of ya'll can go first."

It was raining harder now, and the sun would be up in an hour, so we had to get back to Tom's place before his Ma knew we were gone.

We got out of our wet clothes and into bed and managed to look real sleepy when Tom's Ma came to rouse us about six o'clock to get ready for breakfast. We figured we would lay around in the barn later. We hadn't had much of a chance to compare notes, yet, and were in a sweat for them women to get to work.

We finally got out in the barn to talk. I told the fellers about the food and stuff and Jack said, "Well, over where I was, was clothes and boots."

"Over where I was," Thad reported, "was tents and horses gear and stuff to make camp with."

Tom had the best find of all. "Over on the floor at the southeast corner are crates and crates of rifles." He said, "I didn't see any powder or ball, but them crates were marked rifle, percussion, .50 caliber."

We got to talkin' some more, and Tom says, "Ya' know, no one pays much mind to a kid, so when I get to sweep out taverns and such fer a nickel I hear all kinda stuff. I know there's men in this town'll buy any of them thangs, no questions asked."

"Ya' reckon," asks Jack, "we might could do a little business with 'em?"

"Now wait a minute," says I, "that'd be stealin' an' we cain't do that. Pa'd tan our hides, sure."

"Tag, don't be an ol' lady," said Jack. "Pa ain't here an' it ain't stealin' if we steal from Yankees. They's the enemy, durn yer' sissy soul."

"Jack," says I, "yer skatin' on thin ice. If ya'll want to rob the dang Yankees, count me in, but when we're a standin' on the gallows, and are about to meet the Devil, don't go cryin' 'bout it."

"Even them Yanks devils ain't a goin' ter hang anybody young as us," said Thad. "Why, jeez, we ain't even shavin' yet, though you ort to, Tag, ya' got just enough hair on yer face to make it look dirty."

"Don't you never mind my dirty face, Thad. Just think a minute, fellers…ain't no grown man goin' to give a kid money for rifles. Why, if we could even get a man to believe us, he'd cheat us outta the money, somehow. What we'd have to do, we'd have to show him a sample, and arrange a place for him to pick 'em up. That place'd haf ta be real safe fer us, too, and we'd have ta keep him from knowin' how many of us there was, and keep three of us out in the dark with guns to protect the one that does the dealin'. Then, we'd have to make tracks on outta town, fer he'd be lookin' ta get his money back, and the Yanks would know by then that they'd been robbed. We'd probably have the Yankee Army lookin' fer us as hard as the man we sell to. The onliest way ta do this is ta be real sneaky."

"Well," said Tom, "ya'll been talkin' 'bout goin' out west after cattle, an' I was hopin' ya'll'd ask me along. I ain't got a horse 'er nothin', but I could steal one, if we're a leavin' anyhow. Can I go along?"

"Well, shore," says Jack. "We ain't about ta leave ya' here to face the music after we're gone. Ain't that right, fellers?"

"'Course that's so," says Thad, "but I ain't fer stealin' no horse. I'm fer getting' away from here the same way we came, by river."

"Well, Tom," says I, "since you know what to do, I reckon yer elected to find a buyer, and set a price fer them guns. No paper money. It has to be gold. You tell him to get the gold, and we'll contact him after we got the guns, and tell him where to bring the money. Find out how many rifles he wants, so we'll know how many to take. Whilst yer a doing that, we'll find a good place fer the trade."

Well, Tom went off to try and find a buyer, and the three of us took to walkin' up and down the river banks to see if we could find a safe place for the transfer. We had to have a place that offered cover for three of us, while letting us see the fourth at all times. At this stage of the plan, it was still all a big game to us.

When the day was pretty well shot, we went back to Tom's place, and had supper and then went out to the barn to have a smoke and talk things over. Tom had met a gambler that was in the market for some arms. Tom was to meet with him that night. Tom sneaked out about midnight, and was gone 'til about four in the morning. We were getting right worried about him, when he finally showed up.

"I met that gamblin' feller," Tom began, "down at the Four Aces, an' talked with him a spell, and then these other two gents came and set down. After they talked to the gambler, Doc Collins was his name, for a few minutes, we all went into a little room in the back an' set down around a table. Well, them men grilled me good 'bout who I was and who I was speakin' fer an' all. I lied like hell, an' told them I was paid ten dollars to deliver the message, and that they wouldn't ever see the man who paid me, as he was a Yankee, and didn't want to get caught. They asked me how they could trust a kid, an' I said that ya' don't have to. Alls ya' got to do is tell me how much you'll pay, an' how many rifles ya' want. They told me that they would pay ten dollars, gold, apiece fer them guns, if they was new, and wanted a hunnerd of 'em. I told 'em I'd relay the message, an' that if the price was okay with the other side I'd be back to tell Collins when and where to bring the money and pick up the guns. I bet they're talkin' it over right now, how they're goin' to beat us out of the loot."

"Well," says I, "they durn shore ain't beatin' us outta no loot. We'll make double sure a' that. I been a figgerin' how best ta do this job, an' I come up with a plan. After I tell ya' what it is, ya'll can throw out yer ideas, an' we'll get a real plan together.

First, I think we best do this job whilst it's a rainin'. The guards will likely act like they did last time we was in there. Next, I b'lieve we best steal us some ol' clothes, like the darkies wear, an' rent a wagon with sides on it. What we'll do, we'll lay down a layer a' straw on the wagon bed, an' load the rifles on it. Then, we'll throw a tarp over the guns an' cover the whole load with manure. Ain't no Yank a goin' ta dig through a load a' wet manure, don't ya' see? We'll dark our faces an' hands with burnt cork, an' our feet, too. That way, we'll look like a buncha workin' Nigras ta them Yanks, in the dark like that. Soon's we get outta town, we'll split up an' put our own clothes back on. Tom can drive ta the spot we'll pick and the rest of us will hide in the dark with our guns an' wait. After it's all over, we'll hightail it north to Vicksburg an' get our gear an' get on with ketchin' some cows. That sound all right ta ya'll?" They said it did.

Tom said he'd get the wagon, for he knew a man that owned a livery stable. Ol' Jack, he volunteered to steal the clothes. He was always the sneakiest one of us anyhow.

Bright and early the next morning, we headed south along the river road a lookin' for a likely spot, and found a shallow, little cave just above the river and just off the road, kind of hidden by a little clump of brush. It wasn't deep enough to hide in if a hundred rifles were already in it, which meant that Tom and the buyers would be visible from the bank above the road as well as up and down the river bank. If we made the deal at night, the three of us could hide in the grass and bushes right under their noses.

We went on down to the waterfront to see if we could get passage north. After lookin' at the options, we felt like the best plan would be if Jack and Thad would go on the boat, and me and Tom would go by land

Late that night, after we were sure that Tom's Ma and aunt were fast asleep, we snuck out. Jack and Thad to raid someone's clothesline, and me to find a manure pile. Tom went alone to the Four Aces and told that Gambler, Collins, to have his partners get the gold ready, for the price of ten dollars a gun for a hundred rifles had been approved by the other side. The gambler said he'd pass the word, and Tom came on home.

We had to wait a couple of more days until we got some rain. Good rain for us, for it was a light rain, like a heavy mist, just wet and chilly enough to make a body miserable. We just knew how well them Yankees were a goin' to like guarding a warehouse tonight. They wouldn't hardly be payin' no attention, atall.

All four of us were nervous all dratted day. Ol' Tom, he just kep' a goin' up to his Ma and a talkin' to her and doin' little things for her, and I knew he was a missin' her already. He was plannin' to leave a letter and some gold on his bed when he left. Tom's Ma had been good to the rest of us, so we decided to leave her a little something, too.

Tom went out that afternoon and rented that wagon, and we left it and the team hid down the road 'til midnight. That's when the fun would begin.

We sneaked out of the house that night and put on them stolen clothes. Jack had even managed to thieve us some old straw hats. They were real beat up lookin', and just filled the bill, for we looked like ragamuffins for sure. We got the team and wagon and headed on down to the stable to load up the manure and then made our way down toward the warehouse. We tied the team about a half block from the warehouse and unloaded the manure, covered it and the pitchforks with the tarp and flitted from shadow to shadow on to the back of the building.

Hiding in some bushes near there, we rubbed that burnt cork all over us and got ready to go in. I sneaked up to the front of the warehouse and peeked around the corner to take a look at the guards. Sure enough, there they sat, under the awning lookin' as miserable and put upon as a body can look. They weren't about to move unless an officer came by.

The plan was for Jack and Tom to go inside and start passin' the guns out to me and Thad. We were to carry them, four at a time, back and stack them near the wagon and come back for more. Inside, as each gun crate was emptied, Tom and Jack were to fill them up with some of those airtight tins, and put the lids back on, so's the Yanks wouldn't notice that the rifles was missin'.

We only had to stop work twice when the guards came to the back to take a drink of whiskey or to urinate against the side of the building.

Now each one of them guns weighed about nine pounds and was clumsy to carry, four at a time. When we had the whole hundred of them, we sneaked back to the wagon, loaded them in and covered them with the tarp. Pitchin' all that wet manure on top wasn't no fun, neither.

Tom started drivin' towards the cave, and we all ran down back alleys as quick and quiet as we could to get there before him and make sure the coast was clear to unload.

By the time Tom showed up, I had left Thad up the road a piece, and Jack down a ways to warn me and Tom if anybody came along. Then, we unloaded them rifles and stacked them in that cave, covered with a tarp as snug as a bug. We then cut some brush to hide the mouth of the cave a little better. Satisfied with the job, we went to get Jack and Thad.

We all piled in the wagon, Tom and Jack on the seat, and me and Thad settin' on the tailgate and dangling our legs off the back, like we'd seen field hands do, and rode back into town and on down to the livery stable. We left the wagon beside the barn, unhitched the horses, leaving the leather in the wagon box.

We took turns bathin' in the horse trough, and put our own clothes back on. Jack threw the stolen ones down an outhouse behind one of the taverns.

Tom went on down to the Four Aces and set it up with Collins to turn over the guns the next night at midnight. We all went home and had just fallen asleep when Tom's Ma came to wake us for breakfast.

We napped in the barn most of the day, so's we'd be wide awake that midnight. Restless and nervous all day, we had to make like nothing was wrong, so's Tom's Ma wouldn't get wise to us.

We left the house about ten o'clock that night, and Thad, Jack and I went on down to the cave. I laid out our posts so as to let us cover the cave mouth in a cross fire in case of treachery on the part of the buyers, for common sense told us that they weren't going to want to pay up. There wasn't any way the buyers could know the location of the rifles 'til Tom showed them, but we got into position anyway. Jack was across the road and up a little way, 'bout seventy five feet, and in a little cleft of rock. I cut a bush and put it on him, and you would have had to step on him before you knowed he was there.

I put Thad the farthest away, about a hundred feet, in a shallow hole we'd scooped out earlier and weaved some vines and brush around him 'til he looked like he'd been there for years. The plan was that I would back off a ways to see if Tom and the buyers followed. We knew which way Tom was going to bring them in, so when I heard the jingle of harness, I whistled low, like a night hawk, to let Jack and Thad know to get ready.

I heard a horse snort, and sure enough, here they came. Tom was sittin' beside a big man, and another man was ridin' a horseback beside the wagon. They passed within ten feet of me and didn't even know I was there, I was so quiet. I laid there in the weeds, and in a few minutes, along came two more men a horseback. When they saw the wagon stop, one rode up the hill a ways to circle around to scout around, I reckon, for the other one dismounted and started walkin' toward the wagon.

I crept up on the man and stuck my pistol in his ear. He like to jumped out of his skin when I whispered, "Make a sound an' you get to meet Jesus tonight."

Well, at that, he froze and I whacked him in the head with a rock I had picked up, and he dropped without a sound. He was still a breathin', so I cut strips from his coat to bind and gag him. I put his pistol in the waist of my pants and went off to find the other man. I ran, quiet as I could, up the hill to circle around the wagon, facing away, to try to spot him before he saw me. He was good, too, for he was almost on me before I saw him. If he hadn't sniffed his nose, he would of got by me. I just stuck the pistol in his back and marched him toward the wagon.

We were about a hundred fifty feet away from the cave when I heard a gunshot, and a yell. Another gunshot boomed out, and I thought the jig was up. I pushed my captive faster, until I could see in the circle of light cast by the lantern they'd used when they counted the rifles. Both of the buyers had their hands in the air, and Thad was standin' behind them and Tom was lyin' on the ground, holdin' his head and moanin'.

"You two lay down on yer bellies," I said, "and lock yer fingers together behind yer necks." I prodded my captive in the back with my pistol. "You, too."

"Step in there and take their weapons," I said to Thad. "Don't miss nothin', an' don't get between them and my gunsight."

Thad disarmed the men and found two pistols, a Derringer and a big knife on them along with a little hideout pistol in one of the guy's boot. After collecting the weapons, Thad moved clear and took a look at Tom's head. Tom had a nasty gash above his left eye where the big man had hit and cut him. Tom still had the poke of gold coins in his hand.

What happened was that Jack and Thad had each fired a shot at the men's feet, and didn't have to kill either one of them.

"They was sure enough gonna take the gold back," said Tom. "I still got her, though." At least he had the presence of mind not to use names, for we had talked about that. I held my gun on them varmints while Thad bandaged Tom's head. Jack was tying up the captives and goin' through their pockets. He couldn't see not robbin' them, seein' as how they tried to cheat us first.

We turned the saddle horses loose and left them polecats tied up right there with a team and a load of Yankee guns and not a penny in their pockets. Thad threw all the weapons in the river except for one pistol and holster, that we kept for Tom. We kept the cylinders out of the other guns, too, for we could use them. Well, sir, we hit for home as fast as would sneak through the Yankees. We had a lot to do and a long way to go before daylight. I don't know if them fellers got away with the guns or not, because we left before we heard the end of it.

We got back to Tom's place and cleaned his wound real careful, left the letter and two hundred dollars in gold on his pillow and then left the same way we arrived; in the dark. I thought I saw a tear in Tom's eye when he passed his Ma's bedroom on the way out. Jack and Thad headed for the river, and me and Tom headed for the stage stop, just out of town. We had breakfast at the stop while we waited for the stage, but Tom didn't seem to be very hungry. I was ravenous after all that work, now that the excitement was winding down.

While we sat there, waiting, I looked over at Tom's bandaged head and felt right sorry for him. I knew he didn't want to leave his Ma. If I had one, I don't expect I'd want to leave her, neither. I've always envied folks who had a Ma. Our Pa did the best he could, I reckon, but sometimes, there just ain't no substitute for a Ma. Tom had fixed it so's he didn't have no choice but to leave, if he wanted to stay alive and out of prison. If those men got away, they'd be a lookin' for us for a long, long time.

CHAPTER SEVEN

We had stopped on the way out this morning and bought a Tom a pair of saddlebags like mine. They were a lot handier to carry your gear in than a tow sack. You can sling them over your shoulder so they're real easy to carry along. When I heard them bring the coach around, I stood up, got my saddlebags and went out the door with Tom right behind me. It was drizzling rain and right clammy, too, and the team was splashin' water with their hooves as the driver pulled around the corner of the building. Besides the mail and a drummer selling notions, we were the only passengers.

We boarded, and Tom sat down next to me with the drummer facing us across the aisle. It was a rough accommodation. The leather flaps had been let down to keep the rain out. It was stuffy inside, and dark, too. The worst thing was that we couldn't see out, which made us right uncomfortable, what with people maybe a lookin' for us and all. I didn't have any intention of riding in a contraption I couldn't see out of, so I leaned over and rolled the flap up on my side, and Tom did the same on the other side. The drummer started complaining about how wet we were a goin' to get. I didn't think we could be any more miserable than we already were, and I told him so.

I don't know if you've traveled by coach. I never had 'til then and thought it would be wonderful just to ride along without havin' to pay attention to where you were goin' and not havin' to pay no mind to a fool horse. I surely was wrong, for coach travel rates right up there with a ride in a butter churn, if you ask me.

Them coaches were suspended on leather straps that was supposed to take most of the shock out of the ride, but what they did was to give the coach a ride like a rowboat in a typhoon. The coach would get to swayin' a certain way and then hit a bump or hole in the road and like to jar the eyeteeth outta your head.

If you had a pair of wooden choppers, like ol' George Washington, I bet they'd fly right out of your mouth. There was nothin' to do, and you couldn't see a whole lot, neither. The only good thing was that we were relatively dry, even with the side curtains open. The drummer was tryin' to take a nap, so I thought I'd giver 'er a try, too.

Couldn't do it, though. If you shut your eyes for too long, you got a funny, sick feeling in your belly. We were flappin' around too much to sleep, anyway. All in all, I guess that coach ride was a good one, from what I found out later. Out west, they don't even have roads. That really gives you a fun ride. When that coach stopped for dinner, bout noon, I felt like I had been beat with a stick and Tom said he did, too. I don't know how that fat drummer managed to nap through most of it, unless that little bottle he kept nippin' at helped him along, a mite.

We had made about twenty miles by noon, which wasn't too bad considering that the team had to pull through mud and still maintain a good clip. The team had four horses in it, and was pullin' a heavy load, so five miles an hour wasn't too bad. It was about the same, or pretty near, as a steamboat goin' upstream, if you counted the boats stops as travel time. The teams got changed at almost every stop, so the travel time was pretty uniform, 'til you have hills to pull. Mostly they moved at a trot. For most of the way, the road paralleled the river, but when it could, cut from one river bend to the next, so as to save a lot of time. At the end of the first day, I knew I didn't want to travel by coach anymore than I absolutely had to. It was just too rough on a body, and way too borin' for a young man.

We stopped for the night at a little village called Sorrento, or something like that, after fifty miles, or about two-thirds of the way to Baton Rouge. As soon as we got off the stage, I started walkin' around to get the kinks out of myself. Tom came along, and we walked a little ways towards the river. With the drummer in the coach, we couldn't talk too much, and didn't dast mention anything about what we'd done. While we walked around, we thought we'd see if the hostler for the coach company might have a couple of horses for sale. If we rode, we could take off cross country and save a heap of time, getting to Vicksburg.

Me and Tom walked back to the depot, and went inside in time to have supper. It was beans with ham hock, and cornpone and honey, and fried potatoes, with apple pie for dessert. It being fall, the apples were just startin' to come on. All in all, it wasn't a bad meal. After supper, we stood outside and smoked our pipes, and waited for the hostler to finish supper and come outside. We wanted to ask about some horses.

He finally came out, so we asked him what he had for sale, and he took us around back to the corrals by the stable, and showed us the stock he had. There were half a dozen in there, but only three that might make a halfway decent mount. We stood there and looked for a while and went in among them and threw a noose around the necks of the three likeliest ones and led them out to look over. One of them was in good shape and well set up, but was blind in one eye, so we turned him back into the corral. The other two were tough lookin' little Mustangs, and the hostler told us came from over in Texas.

He said, "Them little fellers was lost in a card game by the man who owned them. He came over to New Orleans from Texas with some cows to sell, and just had to have a ride on a riverboat. Well, Sir, he got in a game with a riverboat gambler and lost all his money, and then bet them horses. They been raised over in that rough Texas country."

I reckon he held us up a mite, but we bought them ponies for thirty dollars each. The hostler didn't have saddles, but he did throw in two bridles and bits. Tom would have to get used to ridin' with just a blanket between him and the horse. Paid him off in Confederate money, too.

We stayed at the depot that night, and after breakfast the next morning, we went and got our horses, and put on the bridles, tossed the blankets on their backs, put the saddlebags on and got ready to mount. I'd noticed Tom watchin' me, to see what I was goin' to do, but I had forgotten about him being a city kid 'til I jumped up on my mount and turned around. I looked over, and Tom hadn't mounted yet.

He looks up at me a settin' there on that little brown horse and says, "I don't know how to ride a horse real well. I don't guess I know how to get on without a saddle or a mounting block."

I didn't know what to say to that, so I joked with him, some. "Well," I said, "I don't reckon we'll be findin' too many mounting blocks where we're goin', so I 'spect I'd better give you a ridin' lesson."

Well, I dismounted by bringing in my right leg over the horse's back and just sliding off. I hitched the pony to the post and walked over for Tom's first riding lesson.

"Well," I says, "if you ain't rode bareback, I s'pect there's things you ought to know 'fore ya' get on. First, it ain't too hard. Don't be ascared of the horse."

Ol' Tom was ready to give 'er a try, so I stood back to watch. Tom grabbed himself a handful of mane and jumped, just like I told him. Trouble is he didn't jump high enough and splatted into the side of that horse, full force. Well, the pony stepped sideways, and ol' Tom fell in the mud at the horses' feet. Of course, he got stepped on. He didn't turn loose of the reins, though. I have to give him that. The next time he tried to mount, he jumped too hard and sailed right on over that pony's back like he had wings. He landed in the mud on the other side, and got kicked, this time. Well, ol' Tom is getting right upset by now. He's breathin' hard and his face is real red. With that red hair and them freckles, he looked like a big carrot. The third time, he lands in the right place, but the blanket wasn't under him, so I handed it up to him and let him arrange it without gettin' off the horse.

Tom looked at me and said, "Durn you, Tag, don't laugh. Let's get goin'. They must be five people a laughin' out the winder at me now. Let's us just get outta here."

I chuckled to myself as we trotted on down the road. Them ponies surely did have a rough trot.

Me and Tom trotted on into Sorrento and tied up in front of the general store. We needed some gear and supplies for the trail, so we went shoppin'. We bought a small coffee pot and some coffee beans, two tin cups, two tin plates, smoked meat, salted beef, dried apples and some penny candy. We got four small tarps that were oiled to repel water, two blankets, some fish line, hooks, some leather thongs, some corn meal, a hat for Tom, two canteens, some Lucifer match sticks, half a dozen candles, lye soap, two towels, a fry pan, two spoons, a little pot, some powder and ball, percussion caps, and four flour sacks to carry it in. While we were in there, I bought my first razor. I'd been lookin' like my face was dirty. The guys were right.

We split the loot into four piles that weighed about the same, and loaded the stuff in those flour sacks and tied two tops together with the leather thongs, so one sack would hang down each side of the horses. The tarps and blankets, we made into bedrolls right there and tied them with thongs, too. Them we tied over our saddlebags with some more thongs. We also bought come cleaning equipment for Tom's pistol, along with the powder measure. We got a little can of grease, too, so we could load those extra cylinders and seal the balls. We loaded the animals and jumped on.

We headed north and stopped for a noon break near the river at Baton Rouge and rode clear on up near St. Francisville before making camp for the night. It had been a long, hard day for the horses and for us, too. I was as stiff as a board when I dismounted, but ol' Tom fell. His legs just wouldn't hold him up.

He said, "I cain't even get my knees together. Why, I'm so bowlegged I couldn't turn a pig in an alley. My thighs are on fire, and that salty horse sweat burns like Hades."

I guess a fifty mile bareback ride was too much for him. I was kind of toughened to hard ridin', but I kept forgettin' that Tom was a city boy. He laid out his bedroll, and I said that I'd make camp. He did gather the wood for a little fire, though. We figured that movin' around would keep him from getting' too stiff. I felt right sorry for him.

While the water was boiling for coffee, we ground some beans with a couple of rocks and heated some salted beef and made some pan bread, for we were plumb starved. After chuck, we laid out our ground tarps and unrolled our blankets. I was to take the first watch, so Tom turned in. He was asleep as soon as his head hit the boots he was usin' for a pillow. Poor ol' Tom was so tired that I stayed awake for an extra two hours before wakin' him for his turn on watch. He was so stiff it took five minutes for him to sit up and pull his boots on.

I waited 'til he had a cup of coffee in him to be sure that he'd stay awake until daylight before I turned in. I had moved my bedroll out in the trees away from the fire so as not to be too easily found if we had unexpected guests. I didn't want another confrontation like Thad, Jack and I had with them deserters.

I woke up about four in the mornin' to let Tom get another two hours sleep before breakin' camp. The day was kind of overcast, but it wasn't raining, thanks be to Jesus. Unless you can find a cave, it ain't no fun to camp out in the rain.

Tom was awful stiff, and I heard him groan when he tried to get on his horse. He didn't make it the first try, so Tom led the pony over to a log and just stepped aboard. It took two hours of slow riding before Tom felt like enough of a white man to talk very much. I was perverse enough not to want Tom to know just how much misery I was in. One man always wants the other men to think he's real hard and nothin' bothers him. It's kind of a code. Stupid, ain't it?

We only rode about thirty five miles that day, up to Woodville. We had to leave the river in order to avoid Fort Adams, for we didn't know if it was in Union or Confederate hands. We stopped in town to buy some supplies and stayed on to get a room in a boarding house and take a bath. We were too durn tired and dirty to want to camp out if we didn't have to. We had a real good meal and slept in a real bed. Ol' Tom had stayed out overnight on islands in the river and such, but this was the first time he'd really had to rough it. He was a trooper, though, and adapted to our wild ways a lot faster than I thought he could. He was pretty tough, for a city boy, ol' Tom was.

All the time we'd been ridin', I had been coaching Tom on horsemanship and why we did what we did on the trail. Me and Jack weren't Indians, yet, but Pa had been keepin' us out in the woods at night since we were old enough to stop wearing three cornered pants, which was what Pa called diapers.

Tom remembered real well, and didn't seem to mind that I was the teacher as some boys would have, us being so near the same age, and all. I had him practicing with his knives, too, and was starting to teach him how to fight with them. He was learning to throw pretty well, too. Pa tried to teach me and Jack everything he had learned in Texas and Mexico, and I was trying to pass it on to Tom. The times he liked best, though, was pistol practice. I didn't have my gun belt with me, so I cut Tom's down like I had mine, and told him why. He dearly loved to draw and fire, and sometimes he even hit the target.

We only made thirty miles the next day, crossing the Homochitto River and riding into Sibley, where we got a room in a hotel. The next morning, we rode on in to Natchez, and got ourselves a room. We didn't have a bit of trouble getting into Natchez. I had thought we might run into a passel of soldiers, but we didn't see a blessed one. It almost seemed like there wasn't any war on, for the only soldiers we saw were on the street. I told Tom we ought to take a nap in the afternoon, so's we could go out that night. I kind of wanted to get a favor or two from them gals again, and besides, we might run into Thad and Jack.

I didn't have any idea where they might be, so we planned to lay around town for a couple of days to see if they would show up. If they didn't, we'd head on up to Vicksburg.

It was a getting on to the first part of November now, and getting a lot chillier in the mornings, and the further north we got, the colder it was going to get. I had hoped to winter in New Orleans, but since that wasn't a good idea anymore, I was hoping for Vicksburg. Adventures and traveling around is great fun when the weather's good, but when the wind howls and the frost is on the punkins, a body just naturally likes to find a snug room and a warm fire. We knew it would be spendy, but we wanted to winter in a city before leavin' for Texas in the early spring.

We went down to the store and got some new socks and underwear, and went to the bath house to bathe, for we didn't want to be dirty if we decided to buy some favors from the gals down at the tavern.

We lay around Natchez for two days before Thad and Jack showed up. Their boat trip was uneventful, except Jack won twenty dollars in a knife throwing contest he'd got started up. We only had time for a meal together before they had to get back to the boat for the next leg of their trip. I told Jack not to get into any trouble and he said, "The onliest trouble I'd like to get into is a red headed gal that gambles with the men. She's wonderful lookin', but even if she sold favors, I don't reckon I'd have enough gold to buy some. Gawd, sometimes I wisht I was ten years older."

Me and Tom lit out the next morning, early, and rode hard to Fort Gibson, for there was lots of soldiers around, and I was ascared of running into any more deserters.

Now, I know that it is dishonorable to desert when you're a soldier, but I can almost see why some do. A lot of the soldiers were in the army to get away from home or else had the law a chasing them back where they came from. Many of them couldn't stand the discipline, and some were downright criminals, and I knew that for a fact. I still dreamed about them fellers I'd had to shoot, and I didn't want to have to do that again for a while, if I could get out of it. Shooting folks puts a feller off his feed for a while. You keep waking up in the night, jerking your hand to your hip reaching for your gun, and seeing the disbelief in their eyes change to horror when they realize they're dying. Crooks don't mind doing you dirt, but when it backlashes on 'em, they want a little mercy from you. Seems real strange to me.

I couldn't talk to my brother or to Thad about such things, for they always said, "Ya' think too much, Tag, an' it ain't good fer a feller." Shooting them men made me give a power of thought to getting shot again myself, and I didn't want to turn sissy if I was too slow on the draw. I think a lot of men, if not all of them, push that hard face so much because, deep inside, they're a little afraid and don't want to admit it. At least to another man. It just ain't proper.

We got into Port Gibson pretty late, and couldn't find any room at the hotel, so we put up without supper in the livery stable's hayloft. We chewed a little jerky that we had in our saddlebags. We were so tired that even the hay felt like a good bed. Sometimes during the night we would wake to a horse stampin' or a mouse rustlin' around in the hay. Tom said he didn't want to get mouse-bit, but I was so tired that I didn't give a durn.

When we woke up the next morning, we washed our faces in the horse trough and slicked down our hair and then took turns brushing the hay off of each other so we wouldn't look too bad when we went to find something to eat.

After eating, we got the horses and gear, and headed out for Vicksburg. There was lots of Yankee activity in this whole area. The Confederate units were scattered, and were working a harassing action against the Federals, with feints here and there. They were attempting to keep the Yanks from being able to mass a large force. The Confederate soldiers were excellent guerillas, striking in small units, here and there, sometimes many miles apart, so the Federal troops couldn't estimate the strength of forces in any one area. This worked so well that the northern troops often thought they were outnumbered even when the Yanks were actually the superior force. The Yankees just didn't know where to consolidate their forces. Both sides were real nervous, and I sure didn't want to be caught between them, so we took our time riding from here on in to Vicksburg. We dodged every horseman we saw.

It took two whole days to cover those thirty five miles, and we slipped into Vicksburg after dark. Vicksburg was solidly Southern. It sure felt good to be safe among home folks, not a durned Yankee in sight, and we didn't have to keep checking our back trail.

That's not to say there weren't a lot of roughnecks and crooks in Vicksburg, just that we felt at home there. 'Course, Pa didn't raise no fools, and even though sometimes we acted like fools, we didn't really trust anyone.

We took the horses to the same stable we had used last time we were here, and rubbed them down good. We paid the night boy, and decided to wait until tomorrow to reclaim our gear from the owner.

We found a room for the night, and got a much needed rest. We would try to find Jack and Thad in the morning. I know they had changed boats in Port Gibson, and the plan was for them to walk or catch a ride in a wagon the last little way so as to dodge any troops, gray or blue, and sneak into the city after dark. 'Course where Jack is concerned, you never knew what he was going to do.

We checked in with the stableman the next morning, and he told us, "I ain't seen hide nor hair of yer brother. If he's to come here, I'll tell him where you fellers are stayin'. I got yer gear safe an' sound, back in the tack room. I got to tell ya', though, I put that red hoss o'yourn out to stud and made seventy-five dollars off'n him since you been gone. Seems like once folks found out that stud came from ol' man Gaines herd, they was just a standin' in line with mares to service. I figgerd ya' wouldn't mind hard money, so I rented him out. I expect to collect twenty-five percent for handlin' it fer ya' and I'll take it off the board bill. I expect you got some money comin' back from that deposit you gave me, so I'll figger it up and we'll settle accounts when ya' decide to leave. I got some more customers fer yer hoss, if yer goin' ta be around yet awhile."

When we'd been in Vicksburg three days and Jack and Thad hadn't showed up yet, I got real worried. For all I knew, they could be in a Yankee prison, or their boat could have sunk or anything. I didn't even have an idea where to start lookin' for them. Tom didn't have no ideas, either. We checked with the army, and they hadn't heard of any accidents or had any reports of any dead folks. I guessed we'd just have to wait it out. We planned to sneak out and go back to Port Gibson and try to trail them from there if they didn't show up in one more day.

Tom and I had gone back to the stable the next afternoon to dicker for a saddle for Tom and get our gear ready to leave for Port Gibson the next morning, when a spring wagon showed up outside with Thad up beside the Negro driver, and Jack on a pallet in the back. He looked to be in pain, but was asleep.

"Thad," I said, "dad gum it, I'm glad to see ya'. I been worried sick. Me and Tom was just getting' ready to go to look fer ya'. What in the devil happened to my brother?"

"I didn't see it, myself", Tag says, "but Mose here did, so I reckon I'll let him tell ya'."

"Well, Suh," says Mose, "my Master and his little gal come into town, Port Gibson, Suh, in this yere wagon, with me a ridin' in the back. We was down by the boat landin', Suh. Me an' the Master was gettin' some bales o' canvas cloth ready to load, and had left his little girl on the wagon. Well, Suh, some durn fool was a drinkin' and started shootin' off his gun and spooked the team. They commenced to run off an' dat little girl was a screamin' fer her Pa. Mr. Jack, thar', he seen it all, an' jumped off'n that big boat an' grabbed them runaway hosses by the headstalls an' brung 'em 'round in a tight turn an' slowed 'em down. Jist when they was almost stopped, the headstall broke, and Mr. Jack fell down an' the wheel of the wagon runned over his laig an' broke it. Mr. Jack he never let out a peep. He hollered at one of them white men to git that little gal down off'n the wagon. My Master, Colonel Maxwell, come a runnin' up and seen what shape Mr. Jack was in an' had a doctor come down an' fix his laig. Colonel Maxwell, he had me load Mr. Jack in the wagon an' carry him out to the plantation. Him an' Mr. Thad, they been out at Sans Souci since the accident. That Mr. Jack, Suh, he be a hero to all the folks. Miss Amanda, the Master's little girl, she's right well thought of by everyone. Special by the Nigras, Suh. I'm right proud to of been of help to Mr. Jack."

"Mose," I says, "I'm obliged to ya' fer' lookin; after my brother. An' when ya' get back ta yer plantation, give my regards to the Colonel, an' express my gratitude to him. If you'd drive on over to the roomin' house, I'll take him off yer hands."

We went on over to the room and we all unloaded ol' Jack and put him on his bed. I had taken a ground floor room so he wouldn't have to go up or down any stairs when he went to eat or go to the outhouse. I knew Jack wouldn't like to use a chamber pot. Jack was tryin' to be jolly, but I knew he hurt pretty bad with all that jouncing around in a wagon for two days and thirty-five miles. Jack said the Doc told him to stay off that leg for four weeks, and to tighten the splints when they felt loose. He was to keep the splints on for at least six weeks. It was a durn good thing that we had decided to winter in Vicksburg. Jack would have had a rough time of it out on the Texas plains.

Well, with Jack's leg broken in two places below the knee, I knew we wouldn't be leaving town anytime soon. Not until after the first of the year, anyway. Really, the first was too soon, anyhow, considering the winter and Jack would need some more time to build up the strength in his leg again. I figured that the best we could do would be to plan on heading west about the middle of March.

That being the case, I found a shack on the outskirts of town to rent for a while. It sure beat paying rent at a roomin' house, and it had a shed and small corral to put the horses in. I did leave the stud at the stable, though. Might as well have some sort of an income, and stud fees were better than nothin'. Tom found a little black gal that would clean and cook supper for us for not too much money, so we hired her. The old lady that owned Sally let her earn money on the side so she could buy her freedom someday.

We didn't do much for the next few weeks except fish and practice with our guns and knives. We worked the ponies, some, to toughen them up for next spring. The more I rode that red stud, the more I liked him. He had a smooth trot and could run like the blazes. We all spent a lot of the time with animals, and I finally taught my stud, Red, to come to my whistle. It was nice to see him gallop across the pasture when I whistled him up. I treated him and coaxed him to come with a piece of apple or a lump of sugar, so it wasn't too hard to teach him. He was smart.

A good part of the time, we were just bored. There is only so much to do in a town, and when the novelty wore off, you bored fast when you were young. We didn't want to spend much money, so we didn't spend much on drinkin' and carousin' around, but sometimes we would go and buy some favors. I must have fallen in love a half dozen times. Lordy, I did like the ladies. All of us did. A couple of times, we prevailed on one of the 'soiled doves' to pay ol' Jack a visit. That sure cheered him up.

Finally, about mid December, Jack took his splints off. He limped a good deal and Tom cut him a stick to help him when his leg got too tired. Jack spent as much time on his feet as he could so as to strengthen the bad leg. When he first took the splints off, that leg wasn't much more than half as big as his good one. Sure was funny lookin.'

Though we mostly spent our time associating with each other, we did meet some of the boys in town. We went fishin' with them and some times one of them would ride with us, if he had a mount, but we really didn't have much in common with the town folks our age. We acted more like grown men. I reckon it was because we didn't have anyone to do for us, so we were a little more responsible, and were old for our ages. After all, how many kids our age had done what we had done? Maybe some Indian kid, but no one we knew, so we were real different than most of them.

While we were staying here, I decided to try shaving. I hadn't done it before for fear that the guys would josh me about it some. I got a piece of soap and a little looking glass I had bought, and went down by the river alone, so the guys wouldn't watch, and shaved. Shaving with a straight razor isn't exactly as easy as your Pa makes it look. The hair on my face was dark and real downy and hard to cut off. I lathered up my face and squinted into that little glass and commenced to skin myself. I must have cut myself a dozen times. I had that razor so sharp, I couldn't feel the nicks. I just noticed that I was finding more and more pink foam each time I made a stroke and rinsed the razor. I finally got the shaving part done, and rinsed my face in the river. I had bought a little bottle of bay rum and splashed some of that on my face like they do it at the barber, and boy, howdy, it did sting. Them cuts were on fire. It like to brought tears to my eyes. Made me pretty near quit bleeding, though. I was a moanin' and fidgitin' around something fierce.

I was right glad that I hadn't tried to shave with them jackasses I ran with a watching. I would of never lived it down. I knew what I was getting into, now, and would shave alone until I got it right. I sure didn't want to think about having to do this all the rest of my life. I guessed that when my whiskers got thick enough not to look stupid, I'd grow myself a beard and moustache. No wonder the roughnecks never shaved.

When I got back to the shack, them jackasses hoorawed me bad. Thad said, "Tag, you look like you lost a scuffle with a pack of wildcats."

"Wild kitties," Jack giggled, "I b'lieve ol' Tag was a playin' Indian an' couldn't find anyone else to cut up, so he was a practicin' on hisself."

They just brayed like the bunch of jackasses I called them. A man can't do a durned thing without folks a makin' fun of him, seems like. I figured to get even with them when they started to grow up a mite and shave.

It was gettin' on toward the end of December, and all of us were feelin' a little down, not being able to go home for Christmas, and all. There wouldn't be any big dinner for us this year. Tom couldn't go back to New Orleans, and there were too many Yankees between the rest of us and home to even think about goin', so we were struck right here in Vicksburg. The Federals had been out in force, and it wasn't safe to go out of town anymore. The Yankees had been making probes at the defenses around Vicksburg for a couple of weeks, now and the Confederate troops expected an attack shortly.

On Christmas morning, I sneaked out of the house and went out to the barn. I had slipped around and bought the gang a present each. I had found a leatherworker and had a pair of heavy, fur lined gloves made for each of them. A feller's hands get mighty cold a ridin' around in the winter time. I didn't know it, but they had planned for Christmas, too. We had all gotten a gift for each other. It was real touching.

Men aren't very imaginative, so each one of us bought four of the same kind of gift. I guess it was so everyone got the same thing from each of us, and no one got slighted. I gave the gloves, and Tom got everyone of us a neck scarf made out of wool. I think they're called mufflers, nowadays. Thad gave us all oilskin slickers, and Jack got us leather leggings that went up and buckled around our waist. He said he was talkin' to a feller who had been out West and seen the Mexicans wearin' them. Jack figured that if we were going cow hunting in the brush and tangles, we could use them. That was uncommon good sense, for Jack.

Jack got us some leather ropes he called La Riatas, too. He said that a feller had said we'd need them to catch cows. That was uncommon good sense, too. That Texican that told Jack all this showed him how to use them lariats, too. It would take a heap of practice to be able to rope anything, but we had a heap of time. Sally, the colored housekeeper, cooked Christmas supper for us, so it was a right nice day after all.

Vicksburg, like I told you before, was just full of caves and holes and declivities and swales. The Confederate Army had used these to good advantage, by putting infirmaries, stables, barracks and such in them. They had made shelters for townsfolks, too. The ammunition was stored in them, and fighting positions were there, too. There were lots of cannon and littler field pieces. There were a great many troops stationed there for Vicksburg was a real fortress. Morale was high, and people were excited about the expected Federal attack 'cause they wanted to get a close up look at the war. Except for Tom, we had seen a battlefield, and weren't too anxious to see another one if we couldn't be a part of the battle. Well, the people of Vicksburg got their excitement, alright. On December 29, Federal troops under that Yankee General, Sherman, attacked.

The attack wasn't a big surprise or anything like that, and the Confederate troops were ready, but a good part of the people, us included, didn't know when it was going to start, and thought the opening cannon fire was distant thunder. As soon as we realized that it wasn't weather, everyone that could rushed towards the sound to see what was going on. The Federals had opened fire with cannon and fired for about fifteen minutes, and then attacked with infantry and cavalry. Wave after wave of bluecoats advanced. Looked to me like there wasn't no end to 'em.

All that shouting and gunfire made a roar that all blended together until no one sound could be distinguished from another. You never heard such a noise. Powder smoke looked like fog as it hung over the battlefield, and bullets and cannonballs were falling all over. Anyone with a lick of sense would of hunted a hole. 'Course, us boys never had a lick of sense. Every so often, a charge toward town would be made, and the Confederate troops would rush out to meet it. The Confederate troops were dug in so well that the Yanks would have had to pull them out of their positions one by one at a horrible cost in Yankee lives. There wasn't enough of 'em in Mississippi to take Vicksburg.

General Sherman took a bad, bad lickin'. He got his jaws boxed so good that never again in the war would he attack Southern troops on an equal basis. He would always have numerical superiority or he would not attack. Later in the war, he would march through Georgia, but he never would forget the lesson taught to him at Vicksburg.

Vicksburg was situated on high bluffs, commanding the river, and was on the highest ground around. Batteries of cannon overlooked the river and had been successful in stoppin' Yankee shipping. The battle at Chicasaw Bluffs gave the Union a resounding defeat. Five days earlier, the Union supply base at Holly Springs had been destroyed, and now, Sherman was defeated at Chicasaw Bluffs. Grant, who was the Commander of the Federal Forces in the West, wanted to take Vicksburg and cut the Confederacy in two. The two back to back defeats kind of took the starch out of him. They'd be back, of course, but not for several months.

We got word later that General Lee had whupped the socks off Burnside up in Maryland at Fredericksburg on December 13th. It was the most humiliating defeat that the Army of the Potomac was ever to suffer. The Confederate forces were doing a bang up job of whippin' Yankees, and it sure stuck our craws that they wouldn't let us fight.

There were looters and such trying to rob the dead soldiers' bodies, but the Southern side said they'd shoot anyone they caught doin' it. There wasn't nothin' we wanted from them nohow.

On New Years Eve, we joined the general celebration. The Yankees had been licked good, and the South was winning all over the state. Spirits were high and the ladies of the evening were doing a bang up business in the favors selling department. It was a real celebration. There were lots of free food and drinks to be had, and the taverns stayed open all night long. The next day, we were not in the best of condition, what with aching heads and tired bodies, so we just laid around.

The weather was cold, but not severe, and we were in a sweat to get on over to Texas. We figured that we could get over there and round up some cattle and get them to a city for sale and maybe be back before summer came on, and then go back for some more. It would take a long time to get to Texas, so we decided to lay up someplace when the weather was too bad, and only travel when we could. Young men get in an awful hurry, sometimes. Sometimes it's a good idea, and sometimes it ain't.

CHAPTER EIGHT

We got our gear ready on the night of the third of January, and lit out for cattle country on the fourth. It was cold, but not raining, and we were dressed for it, so we were comfortable enough. We crossed the Mississippi on a ferry, and took a good look at the gun emplacements as we left. It didn't look like a Yankee would get in there 'til Gabriel blew his horn. We were excited to be moving again, and rode at a good pace toward Monroe, Louisiana, about 75 or 80 miles away. We were surprised at the number of Yankee troops, we had to dodge. We thought they were whipped and on their way up North. 'Twasn't so.

It took two days to reach Monroe, and we laid up there a couple of days because Jack's leg wasn't quite strong enough to be in the saddle so much. It was chilly, too, camping out, so we were glad to find a bed inside. Shreveport was a little over a hundred miles away, and it took us five days to make it. The weather was bad, and the creeks and rivers were swollen, making a dry crossing something only to be dreamed of.

We had to stay in Shreveport for a week to wait for the weather to break. I can't say we were too sorry.

It took us two more days to cover the fifty miles on over to Longview, Texas. We laid up there a day and headed southwest. Everywhere we looked, the land seemed to get more desolate. We could see that gettin' those cows wasn't going to be no church social. We had been warned about the Indians and bad men out in these parts and a couple of the men we talked to said that some Indian was going to be right proud of ol' Tom's red scalp, and fond of Thad's blonde one too. They called it "yaller."

Towns were few and far between out there, and when we had a chance to spend a night or two in one, we were thankful. We kept heading west and south, and reached Waco in about a week and a half. We figured to work the area west of there and see what we could turn up. In Waco, we checked around and found a couple of brothers, Mexicans they were, who were familiar with the area. They didn't know what we would want with wild cattle unless we were goin' to skin them for their hides, like most everyone else did. They said the hides were worth more than the cattle were on the hoof.

Now, we had no experience at catchin' wild cattle, but the Morales brothers did. They seemed to be decent folk, and we took them into our confidence. They said the plan was crazy, but when we offered them a dollar a day each, in gold, to help us out for a month, they readily agreed. Ramon, the oldest, was about five foot seven and weighed maybe 130 pounds. His brother, Luis, was an inch or so shorter and ten pounds lighter. They were about our ages, so they fit right in. They had old smoothbore muskets and knives, but no pistols.

Ramon and Luis took us home to meet their parents, who treated us like royalty. They lived in an adobe shack and farmed 40 acres. The farm was in excellent condition, and their two cows were fresh. They raised goats and chickens, too. Supper was the best I'd ever had. The food was plain, just beans and goat meat and chilies made into what they called chili Colorado. It burned all the way down, but was so good, you couldn't stop eatin' like a starved dog. You rolled up a thing called a tortilla and used it like a spoon. It was wonderful.

After supper, we men went out on the front porch and had a smoke and a drink of Aguardiente. It was a hot clear liquor a lot like moonshine the men made back home, and could burn the hair right off your tongue and you could feel the heat all the way down. Anyway, as we talked and walked around lookin' over the farm, Mr. Morales said, "Thees wild cow, Senor Tag, they big as a little horse, an' I theenk you maybe not so good vaquero, no? Con su permiso, with permission, I geeve you some wisdom. Them saddles you got, she's too light for to lasso cow. Light single girth, she break, an' maybe you are keel, an' maybe horse is keel. No place to snub la riata. You got open iron stirrup. No good. Need tapaderos. Is cover over toe so no brush get in. Brush jam boot, out you fall. No good. If you say, I go see mis amigos, find quatro good Mejicano saddle. Big horn, tapaderos, double rig girth. I find for poquito dollar. Leetle money. Mis hijos, my sons, they already got."

I said, "Mr. Morales, I'll take the saddles, and any other advice you got fer us. We don't know nothin' 'bout catchin' wild cattle. We was dependin' on yer boys to help us out there."

Well, that ol' man, he was a sight of help. He told us lots of things we wouldn't have thought of. Like keeping a pistol handy. Not only for an extra mean cow, but because we would be ridin' in Indian country. The area we were goin' to be ridin' was a joint hunting area, used by both Kiowa and Comanche. Both of whom were fierce warriors and not friends of the white man. He warned us not to let ourselves be captured, because both tribes tortured captives to test their courage. Well, that didn't sound like no fun to me, so I vowed not to be caught.

Another thing he told us was to cut all the young bulls and bull calves, and not to try to take any full grown bulls. He said they were just too mean. He also told us to throw and brand every head we took, so no one could steal from us. He said to register the brand, so we did. We chose a rocking chair for a brand. Pa had always said me and Jack were so lazy that we ought to take a rockin' chair to the fields with us, so we wouldn't tire ourselves. Mr. Morales said his hijos, boys, knew what to do since they had gone hide hunting with him a few times.

Early next morning, while Mr. Morales was off finding some saddles, the five of us boys went into town to get a wagon and some provisions. We found a little two wheeled wagon with a box about five feet by seven feet with an oiled canvas top on it for twenty-five dollars in gold. It was owned by a widow woman who needed the money. Luis greased the axles and looked it over real good and pronounced it sturdy enough for what we needed. Ramon and Jack went back to the Morales' farm and got some harness and picked up two of the packhorses to hitch up and see if we couldn't make a team out of them.

Them ponies had never been in harness before, and it was a real circus gettin' them hitched. After a lot of cussin' and pulling and tugging, we got them hitched and after about an hour, could drive them pretty well. We took the wagon down to the general store and bought enough supplies to last six men a month, and loaded them in that little wagon. We figured to kill enough game and beef for meat to eat, so we bought sugar, coffee, flour, salt, corn meal and beans. Like I said before, we lacked imagination.

We also bought a hammer, nails, two shovels, a pick and mattock, and two sickles and some hatchets and an axe. We got a lot of rope for pickets and corrals. We got us some picket pins, too. Some new flint and a steel, and we thought we were well fixed. Ramon said we should get some mescal for disinfecting and we could drink some, too, and it sounded like a right good idea to me. We also stopped at the blacksmith shop and picked up our rockin' chair branding irons.

We took the wagon and all the loot back to the farm. We would be leaving from there in a day or so, but we had plumb forgot pots and pans and buckets and a couple of small water barrels, so we had to go back and get them. We weren't used to setting up housekeeping. We hoped we had it all, now. By the time we got back the second time, Mr. Morales had returned, too. He had gotten saddles, and some decent blankets, too. The tack had been hard used, but was in good shape. Tom said that they would likely get more hard use real soon and he was more right than he knew.

We had a busy day, and thought it would be fittin' if we went into town to celebrate. After supper, we got on our horses and hightailed it in. Luis said, "Most of the gringo saloons won't serve Mexicans, Tag. I know a leetle place down in the Mexican part of town we can go. There won't be no gringos, but maybe so you'll be safe with us. These cantina, she's a rough place, so don't let nobody know if you ascared."

We got there just a little after sundown, and tied the horses to the rail in front. The cantina was an adobe and wood shack with a little sign in front that had a picture of a white horse on it and the words, "Caballo Blanco." Ramon said that it meant white stud horse. Inside were several tables and some chairs and stools. The bar was made of rough lumber, except for the top, which was sanded smooth.

The air was thick with tobacco smoke from little cigarillos and old smells of human bodies, beer and hard liquor. The coal oil lamps were kind of dim and there was an old man playing a guitar while a girl danced on the bar. The dancer was about five feet tall, and was voluptuous. She had flashing black eyes and curly, shoulder length hair. Her lips were full and red, and she was sweating slightly from the exertion of the dance. She was barefoot, and her feet were small and her calves were showing. When she twirled, her skirt would swing out and show her thighs and a little higher.

The men were clapping their hands and laughing and shouting encouragement to her. Other girls were trying to get the mens' attention. Ramon and Luis walked in first, followed by the rest of us. When the Mexicans noticed four white boys walk in, the music stopped, the girl stopped dancing and the laughter and banter died. Everyone was watching us.

We pushed two tables together and sat down with our backs to the wall. Luis walked up to the bar and said, "Dos mescal, por favor." and pointed to some bottles behind the bar. He brought the liquor and some shot glasses back to the table and sat down, pushed his sombrero back, opened the bottles, poured us all a drink, raised his glass and said, "Salud" and took a drink.

We all followed suit and the activity in the cantina slowly started to return to normal. The guitar began a playing and the girl began dancing. Slowly the men again became absorbed in watching and joking. I breathed a sigh of relief. There for a minute, it looked like trouble.

Some of the patrons were obviously farmers, and dressed like Mexican farmers always had. They wore white baggy shirts and pantaloons and had sandals on their feet. Some wore sombreros and others had rags tied around their heads to catch the sweat when they worked. Some had both. Others were ranch hands, it seemed to me. They wore calico shirts, short jackets, pointy boots and flared pants. Some had sashes around their waists instead of belts. Almost all had a knife showing and some had pistols. Most of which were single shot, but there were a few revolvers.

We sat there and talked for quite a while, and every so often, I would hear the word "gringo." Not speaking any Mexican, I asked Ramon what "gringo" meant.

He told me, "Even before the war Santa Ana lost, there were hard feelin's between our peoples. A song your people sang most often was something 'bout 'Green Grow the Lilacs.' We jus' shortened to 'green grow' then to 'gringo.' It is not a good thing to be called."

After a while, a couple of the Mexican gals came over to our table and sat down. I started talking to one, Maria, her name was, and seemed to hit it off pretty well, so she came around and sat on my lap. Now, I had noticed that them little brown gals were well set up, most of them. Well built with full bosoms, round hips and soft looking skin. With their dusky skins and shiny black hair and black flashing eyes, they were lovely. 'Course, they went to fat, a lot of times, when they got into their twenties. After a bit, and a couple of drinks, Maria asked me I wanted to go to her room with her. Of course, I did.

She took me by the hand, and we went out the back door to a shack out back. Not being a trusting soul, I kept my hand on my pistol until she lit a lamp, then I went in the shack and barred the door. The room was clean and neat, with calico curtains on the window, and a cloth on a small table. The chairs had pads on the seats made of some flowered material. There was an oval rag rug on the floor by the bed which was made up with a spread on it. Jesus on a cross hung over the bed. There was a small fireplace built right into a corner of the wall, in the Mexican fashion, that had a small fire going. I guess she used it to cook, too, for there was a covered pot on one hook, over the side of the flame. A wash basin and ewer of water completed the furnishings. All in all it was a nice, cozy room, and I began to relax

I was in there about an hour. I think I fell in love again. It was kinda hard to get a favor what with Jesus a lookin' down on ya' and all. When we returned to the cantina proper, the first thing I saw was a Mexican man, dressed in leather, jerk a gal off Jack's lap, and fling her to the floor. He reached out and slapped Jack hard on the side of his face, and like to knocked Jack off the chair. Then he jumped back a step and called Jack a name in Mexican.

"Hijo de puta," he yelled, "tha's mi mujer, woman."

Jack stood up real slow. There was a red handprint covering his left cheek. The room was deathly quiet. Jack never took his eyes off the man.

"Ramon," asks Jack, "what do ee-hoe day puta mean?"

Ramon whispered, "It mean son of a whore."

All you could hear in the room was your own heart beating when Jack looks right in the Mexican's eyes and says, "Feller, you don't even know my Ma. You got two pistols in that sash. You better go fer one for I aim to shoot ya' where ya' stand."

The Mexican wasn't much older than us, and I guess he didn't think little Jack would take this stance. I ain't sure he wanted anything more than a fist or knife fight, but he didn't know what he was dealing with in Jack. Jack saw our Ma like an angel, and took any slur on her memory real personal.

"I'm a gonna count three, you yellow livered sucker, then I'm gonna do you in," he whispered. The man's eyes darted around and his face lost color. He screamed and went for his gun, but he never even got it out of his sash when Jack's gun roared twice and the Mexican twisted sideways and fell to the dirt floor. Jack stepped up to him and leaned over and took both pistols from the sash, and stepped back. The Mexican was layin' in a ball on his side. Jack had shot him through both shoulders.

"Yer' durn lucky I ain't my brother, feller. He'd a killed ya' sure. I changed my mind. You ain't worth killin'. Get your ass out'n here, an' don't call a man's Ma names no more."

Jack never turned a hair. He went back and sat down like nothin' at all happened. The wounded man's friend helped him out the door. Jack looked at them pistols. They were silver plated and had white grips.

"Guess that feller fancied fine pistols. Look kinder dude

like ter me," Jack opined. He handed one of them to Luis and the other to Ramon.

"You ain't got one a' these, so happy late Christmas."

Jack was a corker, all right.

We figured that was a good time to leave, and while we were riding back to the farm, Luis says, "Jack, I was thinkin' your goose, she was cooked. That Pablo, he a mean one, un hombre malo. I thinkin' you goin' be keel. You got to show me how to use la pistola like that."

"Well," said Jack, "I ain't the fast one. Tag spends a hour a day, at least, practicin' with his pistol. Get him to show ya'. Get ya' some cut down leather, like I wear. It saves a heap a' time, when ya' need yer gun in a hurry." Both Ramon and Luis asked me to show how it was done, and I said I would.

The sun was just coming up when we pulled the team away from the farm. Mr. Morales had had a final word or two of advice for me.

"When you ain' on that caballo rojo, red stud horse, keep heem tie'. Lotsa wil' horse out there, an' he smell them mares, you ain' got no horse no more. Vaya con Dios, Chico."

I waved at him and reined around, touched ol' Red with my spurs, and off we went.

We trailed west and south for three days before we found a likely spot to hunt. The place we stopped was near a little box canyon that had a spring in it, and a mouth maybe fifty yards across. The only way out the back was a steep, rocky path that would be easily blocked. On the way out here, we had seen quite a few head of cattle at a distance and the plan was to round them up a few at a time and herd them into the canyon until we had enough to trail on home.

The canyon had a flat floor, and about a section of ground. It was still winter, though, but there was shelter in some cottonwood trees and enough fodder for a large number of animals for a short period of time. Water was kind of scarce out here, and the spring was used by a goodly number of animals, so we camped well back from it.

We worked in shifts, two of us out scouting and learning the lay of the land, and the other four building a trap of cut brush that winged out from the mouth of the canyon, forming a funnel. We then constructed a gate to close it with. We also dug a ditch from the spring for about a hundred yards to allow more access to the water. Each night, the scouts would report their findings, and I would draw a map marking trails, springs, cover, groups of trees and anything else that we thought important. Also where we had seen the most of the animals hid out in the draws and gullies during the day, and we would have to ride down each and every one of them to chouse the cattle out.

At a distance, the land looked flat as a board, but it was covered with gullies and declivities. Sometimes you would find a little canyon or valley right out on the prairie, absolutely hidden until you rode right to the rim of it. Many of these had their own spring, trees and grass. From the tracks and droppings, you could see that cattle and horses both used them for shelter when it stormed and for water on a regular basis. We planned to use one or two of these for alternate camps if we should be caught in a storm or find more animals than we could herd to the main camp alone.

Ramon and Luis had grown up on the prairie, and knew all about survival out there. You wouldn't think there would be much to it, but there was.

After we got all the early work done, we left Jack and Luis in camp, and the rest of us spread out and kind of used the camp as the hub, and we radiated out like spokes from it. I rode slowly and looked things over well, for we didn't want any accidents or ugly surprises, and this country was full of them. That first morning, I just saw one young cow that was catchable. I was riding down a little draw, and saw her moving away ahead of me, and when she broke out onto the plain, I chased her and finally got her turned. She charged my horse, and he durned near unseated me. If I had not been ridin' that Mexican saddle with the high cantle and horn and them big swells under the pommel, I would have been thrown.

Anyway, the horse turned out of her way, and she went by us like a runaway train. She stopped and looked back and saw us coming and tried to run away again. I spurred after her and got her turned. It was a hard way to herd, and it took me two hours to get that cow back into the canyon. That canyon was only about a fifteen minute ride, if I had been able to go in a straight line.

Somehow you don't think of cows as wild animals, but they can be. Now, you have to remember that these cows weren't your ordinary milk cows. These were big rangy, tough cows that fought with other wild animals for existence. They were fully capable of killing wolves and cougars. They had horns as big as six feet in span, but I can't say I ever saw them. They were nothing to mess with, and if you happened to be unhorsed, you would be in a lot of trouble.

Tom didn't get any cows, but Ramon had four when he came in. He caught two, and then happened upon a cow with an early calf, and brought them all back. Those Morales brothers were Vaqueros, though, and had worked cattle before. I figured that we all better take lessons from them for the next few days. Thad brought back one young bull, and a bloody horse. It wasn't a bad day atall. Six head was a good day, and we had just started, so we were real encouraged.

When I asked Thad how his horse got hurt, he said, "Stupidity on my part, I reckon. I was a ridin' along the edge of one of them little canyons and noticed some cows down in there, and went down to get 'em. That ain't easy as it looks, ya know. I rode up on this one an' found out too late that it was a big ol' bull. I tried to shoo him out of the brush, and he charged me. I was against a hillside, and my horse didn't have much room to move. That big ol' devil of a bull hooked the horse with his horn, and that horse jumped up and landed with his front legs over the bull, and me and the horse slid off his back. Both of us went down, an' the bull seen a way to get past us, and was gone. The last I seen of him, he was a high tailin' it down the valley. Fer as I'm concerned, he can just keep a goin'. I never been so scairt in my life.

After I seen that the horse wasn't hurt too bad, I went on up that little valley, and caught the one I brung in. He give me a devil of a time, but here he is."

Luis and Jack had supper on, and it was right good. Jack had set some snares and had caught four or five rabbits, and Luis had cooked them on sticks over the fire. He and Jack had made some pan bread and hot frijoles.

After supper, we just sat around and talked for a while. Luis and Ramon gave us a quick lesson in wild cow catching. We made up that we would work in two, two man teams, with Luis on one team and Ramon on the other so as to teach us faster. That left two of us in camp to do the chores of cooking, hunting and taking care of the stock. If we were able to corral ten head of cattle a day, we would only have to stay out here a month.

Luis said, "We can no drive more than t'ree honnerd head with six men wha' don't know one en' of the vaca from 'nother en'."

After we turned in, we heard a lot of commotion just outside the gate we had strung. That herd of wild horses we had seen sign of had come to drink and found the gate up and they had to make do with the water from the ditch we dug. Some time during the night, my stud, ol' Red, ran off. He had broken his tie rope off at the halter ring. I guess Mr. Morales was right. I should have hobbled him or something. I had to ride one of the packhorses. Red had spoiled me. The packhorse was a good animal, but none of them had Red's gait or stamina. We found ourselves changing horses at noon because of the hard way we used them. They got tired enough to start stumbling after about four or five hours of "brush poppin", as Ramon called it.

We did catch a sight of cattle, with no major injuries, although we all had a multitude of little hurts. The horses all suffered little cuts, but the Morales brothers doctored them with a sap like medicine they made out of a plant that grew there, and sulphur. They rubbed it in the cuts and scratches and none of them ever got infected, and the flies didn't blow the cuts. Worked real well. Luis said it was the sulphur that did the trick, so I filed that away in my head.

After we had about a hundred head caught, we finally found the time to brand them and cut the bull calves. The Morales boys did most of the ropin' because they were better at it, though we all had had enough practice by now to be fair at it. Luis would single out an animal and get his riata over its horns and drag it into the open where Ramon would rope its back legs and stretch the cow out on her side after she fell over.

We had built a little fire and had gotten the rockin' chair branding irons red hot. After the animal was stretched out on it's side, one of us would run up and lay the red hot iron on the animal's hip for a long count of three, and step back out of the way. When you first put the iron on the animal, it would flinch, and let out a bawl. By then it was over, and you could let them go. The smell of burning hair and hide was fierce. Right stomach churning.

If the animal was a bull, we ran up and made a slice in the back of his scrotum and castrated the poor devil. After removing the testicles, we put a hand full of flour and sulphur mixture in the wound, and then swabbed it with a tar that Mr. Morales had given us. The powder and tar practically stopped the bleeding, and then the bull that was now a steer was ready to turn loose. The whole thing was a messy and smelly job. We branded the steers right after the castration.

It kind of made me queasy to cut the equipment off a male animal. Still does. I'm kind of sissy, I reckon, though in those days, I'd die before letting the others know it bothered me. I expect that they felt the same way, if the truth was to be known. Every time I cut a bull, my own testicles kind of cringed and drew up in sympathy.

Now, bull balls are about as big as your fist, each one of them. The Morales boys called them mountain oysters or fries. They washed the things, cleaned them, rolled them in flour or cornmeal and fried them up for supper. Sliced thin and eaten like steak, them boys wolfed the things down. The rest of the boys seemed to like them, too. I forced myself to eat some and told everyone how good they were, but I was a lyin'. Every time I took a bite, my own balls hurt. I still don't like to eat the durned things.

Luis and I were riding together one day when we came upon a place where there had been a lot of activity by wild horses, and found the carcass of one. Luis got off his pony and walked over to the carcass to look it over. It looked to me to have been killed by wild animals, maybe a wolf pack or a big cat. Prairie wolves are large, vicious animals that hunt in packs and follow the buffalo herds. The carcass was savaged pretty good, so it was a reasonable assumption, I thought.

The rain had washed out most of the tracks, but Luis knelt down and studied the carcass and the surrounding area. After lookin' things over for a while, he said, "These horse, he not be keel by no wolf. He been keel by 'nother stud. Mira, look, him leg, she been broke an' he been stomped good, too." I hadn't even known that horses killed each other, I was that green.

After we had been out on the prairie for about three weeks, Tom and Ramon were out about ten or twelve miles from camp when Ramon spotted a herd of buffalo. Ramon was smart, so he and Tom threw their ponies down and laid across their heads so they couldn't get up. They watched the herd start to run and laid there to watch. Pretty soon, sure enough, they saw that the herd was being chased by a bunch of riders that they made out to be Indians.

When they told us about it, Ramon said, "When the herd, she run lak tha', fer sure los Indios chase. It jus' no good to be ketch by los Indios. Muy malo, ver' bad. Them Indios, they make El Diablo, the devil, look lak sissy. Muy malo. We wait long time, and then ride lak hell."

Tom and I had been working some rough country some little way south of the camp. We planned to pack up in a few more days and go back to Waco, so we weren't looking to get many more cattle. As we were working some of the little draws, we topped out on a rise and saw a herd of wild horses out in a little swale. We didn't want to spook them, so we just sat there and watched. There were a few early foals with their mamas grazing out there. The little ones were so cute looking, it seemed that you could go out there and pet them a while.

Tom finally spotted the stud off a little rise, standing there like a king with the wind blowing his mane, watching his mares. Tom punched his thigh with his fist and said, "Tag, if that ain't ol' Red, I'm blinder'n a damn bat."

Sure enough, it looked like Red, so I gave him a whistle. His head came up and he looked around, so I whistled again, and he spotted me. He came toward me at a gallop and stopped about fifty feet away, snorting and tossing his head like he was Lord of the plains. I dismounted and walked toward him. He was a little spooky, but let me rub his forehead and his nose. When I started to go around to his side, he shied away. I grabbed his halter and held on. He dragged me for a few feet before he stopped like he was trained to do.

I looked over at his mares, which were getting spookier by the minute, rubbed his forehead one more time and turned him loose. He looked at me for a bit, then I slapped him on the side and stood there watching as he ran, kicking up his heels, back to his harem. I stood there with his halter in my hand and watched them go. I liked that horse, but I didn't want to take away his freedom and his harem.

Tom asked, "What'd ya' do that fer? That was a good horse."

I just shrugged and said, "I dunno. Seemed right at the time." and let it go.

We were eating supper that night when I heard a whinny out there on the prairie, so I went over to the gate and whistled real loud. I heard the whinny again and saw that stud coming for me at a dead run. Behind him was a string of some of his mares, so I opened the gate, and after they all ran in, closed it. The mares and some of the foals ran to the far end of the valley, but ol' Red, he stayed right by me. I reckon he missed me or missed his treats. Either way, it was great to have him back.

We sorted them mares the next day, and turned some of the older ones and some scrubs loose. We spent the next ten days getting the ones we kept green broke. The Morales boys were the best riders, so they did most of the work. We branded every head of stock we had with the rockin' chair, even ol' Red. After I slapped that hot iron on him, he wouldn't go near me for two days. He forgave me, though and was as tame as an old hound dog. Even Ramon said that he'd never seen a stud so tame. That ol' red stud had brought us twenty-two mares and a few foals. Red was marked up pretty good, and I thought it was from brush, 'til Luis and Ramon pointed out some bite marks and reminded me about that carcass we found.

"Well," I says, "I reckon we know what killed that ol' stud, don't we."

We broke camp on the first day we'd had in as week that it was clear. It took a long time to get the herd lined out. The wagon left early to find a place to camp and hold the herd for the night. Luis and Ramon were worth their weight in gold, for without them, we would have had to line out that herd one at a time. Ramon let an old cow take the lead. "She the patrona," he said. "Where she go, the rest follow." That's the way it worked, too. It took a few days to get back to Waco, and by then the herd was used to the trail. They followed that old brindle cow like she was their mama. The only time we had much trouble was when we had to cross a river. Some of the herd didn't want to go in the water and we had to force them in with rope ends. We were slowed down some by new calves being born on the trail, and sometimes we'd give them to a farmer if we could. If they couldn't keep up, we had to leave them behind. Jack was so soft hearted, he'd leave the mama behind, too. We all carried the little calves across our saddles or in our arms a time or two.

We held the herd on the banks of the Brazos River, just a little east of Waco, so the Morales boys could go see their folks and pick up the news of the war. We had been out of touch for a month or more, and didn't know what was going on. They were gone over night, and were glad to see their folks. They said that cattle buyers were traveling around to try to find enough beef to feed the armies. No one really wanted to sell to the Yankees, but everyone needed money.

The war was going on full blast in the east. There had been a lot of fighting and word was that Grant still wanted to capture Vicksburg in order to control the whole Mississippi. We talked it over and decided to push the herd hard to Shreveport and sell it. We wanted to slip into Vicksburg and try again to get into the army. We pushed on up toward Tyler and on to the Sabine River, where we had to lay up for a few days to wait for the level of the river to fall so we could ford with some chance of not losing too many head.

While we were in camp at the Sabine, some buyers came out and said that they had had news of the herd and had followed the sign we left 'til they found us. The Confederate Army was in need of beef and they offered to buy the whole herd on the spot, and hold it there until they could bring up their own drovers. We boys talked it over, us being partners, and negotiated a price of ten dollars a head, calves included. We delivered 341 head of beef and got paid in gold coin. The south still had some gold then.

Tom, Thad, Jack and I had a little meeting and decided that even though we had originally hired the Morales boys at day wages, that without them this whole venture would probably not have succeeded. We decided to cut them in for a full share each, after expenses. When we paid them each $500.00 in gold and three of the captured horses each, they were overjoyed. That gold took them right from day laborers to ranchers in one minute. They were going to use the money to buy some land south of Waco and start a ranch. We gave them the wagon and most of the supplies.

After thinking it over, Jack, Thad and I gave the Morales boys all the money we had made in profit on this trip, five hundred dollars each, and our extra horses too. We said that we'd like to be partners with them in the ranch, and made a deal for them to set it up. Tom gave up his share of the horses, but not the gold, for he wanted to send it to his Ma. We shook hands all around. When the boys, Luis and Ramon, had visited home they had brought our army saddles back in the wagon.

We left the heavy Mexican saddles with them to keep for us until we showed up again. We didn't know when that would be. The deal with the Morales boys was done on a handshake. We had no second thoughts about it. We trusted them, and they trusted us. Besides, if we lost all that we had given them, it was only a lot of hard work. We still had a lot of money on us.

We crossed the Sabine and headed for Shreveport. Once there, Tom caught a boat down stream for New Orleans to visit his Ma. We told him to be real careful, fer those gents that we'd had the run-in with might still be around.

Tom said, "After all we've been through, I don't even look the same. My clothes are different and my skin's darker. Kinder hides the freckles. I'll join you fellers in Vicksburg, by n' by. If yer gone, leave word at that same stables where ya' went. Soon or later, I'll show up."

When Tom left, Thad said, "Well, it's back to just us. Seems kinder lonesome, somehow."

It did too. We didn't realize how much of a hole got left in your life when the people you'd risked your life with, and sweated and suffered along side of were gone. We missed the soft voices of Luis and Ramon, and Tom's eternal optimism. I discovered then that in each relationship with another person, you leave something of yourself with them and take something of them with you. Always and forever. At odd times you will think of a person you've not seen for a long time. It's a kind of a strange fact of life.

CHAPTER NINE

The three of us headed towards Vicksburg, and sneaked past some Yankee patrols to get in under the cover of darkness. We were dirty and our hair needed cuttin', and after living out in the open for several months, we were lean and hard. Our faces and hands were weathered and windburned, and we looked a lot older than we were.

We found a Cavalry officer, and told him we were from West Texas and had ridden all the way here to enlist and fight Yankees. He took a look at us and I suppose he hadn't seen civilians as wild lookin' as we were unless they were Indians. He asked about the rockin' chair brands on our horses, and we told him that we were from a ranching family and that was our brand. His name was Jackson, and we asked if he was kin to Stonewall Jackson, but he said he wasn't. He was a Major.

Major Jackson took us to the Colonel commanding, and he swore us in. We were now Confederate private soldiers. We all felt right proud. The Colonel told us that he was sending Major Jackson and a detachment of cavalry to the camp of General John C. Pemberton, the commander of all Confederate forces in the area. There, we would receive training in cavalry basic maneuvers, and tactics, and customs and courtesies. Thad and Jack weren't too keen on all this trainin' stuff. They had thought that we just rode up and shot Yankees. Myself, I was glad that they were going to teach us what we needed to know to stay alive.

Since the cavalry detachment at Vicksburg was small, it was short of horses, so they were glad to hear that we had our own mounts and arms. They gave us uniforms, and made us get rid of the officer's style hats we wore and also the cut down pistol belts. We were issued regulation gear. Major Jackson turned us over to an old sergeant that looked like he was as old as Methuselah. He must have been forty-five or so, and looked a lot older. He was as hard as nails.

We learned in a hurry that there was a lot more to soldiering than we had thought. Sergeant Cates started right away teaching us about customs and courtesies. Yes, Sir, No, Sir, at your command, Sir, if you please, Sir, salute, salute, salute. Follow orders, don't question them. He used his hands and fists, too. After a couple of run ins with him, I didn't have too much trouble conforming. Jack, though, he was right wild, and had to take a few lickings before he saw the light. This training wasn't near as much fun as we had thought it was going to be. We didn't have a minute for ourselves.

Every so often, Sergeant Cates and Jack would go out, and Jack would come back with knots and bruises on him. He wanted to be a soldier real bad though, so he took it. See, the army ain't as easy to get out of as it is to get into. Once they got you, you have to do as they say 'til they turn you loose. If you don't cooperate, they shoot you. Oh, they can lock you up, but in those days the Confederacy was too busy fighting a war to mess with you.

Five days after we joined up, a small contingent of us left for General Pemberton's headquarters. Thad, Jack and I got to do all the chores, us being the new recruits. We took care of 35 horses, gathered wood for cook fires, set up officers' tents, ate last, did up all the dishes, and stood guard duty and slept least.

As Thad put it, "Ain't a slave in the south got it as bad as we do. Slaves say 'Massuh' and we say 'Yes, Sir'…thets the onliest difference."

"Yep," said Jack. "Least wise they get to daince a little. We ain't got time, even, fer thet."

After we arrived at the headquarters, we were introduced to cavalry tactics and drill. We took to that like ducks to water, for after all, we rode real good. We got a basic understanding of tactics by listening to the officers, and more by drilling. Seems like all armies do is drill. Keeps the troops busy, I reckon. Things got a lot better after we got assigned to a regular cavalry company. The duties were lighter, and we spent all our time with the same people. That was to teach us that troops fought as a unit, and except in rare instances, never were alone.

These were the men who would defend and protect you, and you were expected to do the same for them. These soldiers were to become like your family. Like any family, there are disputes, and of course, some of the time, someone just doesn't fit in. There are always bullies, and sometimes they don't know when to quit teasin'. There is a pecking order, and you have to earn your place in it. Your rank only matters to the army. How you are thought of by your peers is what was really important. Were you tough? Were you mean? Were you to be depended on in a fight? No one knows the answers until you have fought. Not only among yourselves, but against the common enemy. All veterans are mean to the new guys, for they are an unknown quantity.

Every new guy must prove himself every time he changes companies or outfits. You constantly prove yourself. The veterans watch you like a hawk. They want to know if you can hold up your end and in a fight, and they won't give you the time of day if they think you don't measure up to their standards. Rightly so.

While we had been getting used to Army life, the Yanks hadn't been idle. Grant had decided that he was a going to take Vicksburg or bust. On April 16th a Yankee Admiral named Porter had been ordered by Grant to run a bunch of ships past Vicksburg. He only lost one transport out of six. On the next night, he lost one transport and five barges out of six barges and thirteen transports.

Grant now had enough transportation to come up the West side of the Mississippi with his troops and cross the river below the range of the guns at Vicksburg, and try to take the city from the rear. Grant crossed to the east bank of the River on April 30, 1863. A week later, he moved on Jackson, the capitol city, and after a short but vicious battle, his forty four thousand troops against only six thousand defenders, took the city. Grant then turned west to try to take Vicksburg from the rear. When Grant's army got to Champion's Hill, about halfway between Jackson and Vicksburg, we were waiting for him. Federal units under McPherson attacked us and I got my introduction to war, up close.

The two armies had formed up on opposite sides of a meadow about a mile and a half long during the night. That meadow was about four hundred yards wide at its widest point and maybe two hundred and fifty at it's narrowest. Knowing there would be a fight, come morning, no one could get any sleep. Thad and I found Jack sitting all by himself, staring out into the darkness.

"Hi, ya', fellers," he said, "I'll tell ya' somethin' if'n ya' promise not ta call me a sissy. Ya'll promise?"

"You bet," says me and Thad.

"I reckon I'm 'bout scared ta death. I been over there a half dozen times, a tryin' ta pee, an' nothin' comes out. I'm breathin' fast, an' cain't eat no supper. Feel like I'm a goin' ter puke, too. I reckon I'm ascared. I'll probably turn chicken when the shootin' starts. Tag, if'n I do, ya' got ta promise ta put a bullet in me, fer I'd a durned sight ruther be dead than be chicken. I couldn't never look at myself in a lookin' glass again, if'n I was chicken."

"Jack," says I, "Sergeant Cates caught me just a lookin' at my supper. I hadn't took more'n two bites and couldn't hardly swaller. He come up an' put his hand on my shoulder an' said 'A soldier wouldn't be in his right mind if'n he warn't a little ascared before a battle.' He said 'It ain't bein' a scairt that counts; it's not doin' yer duty that makes ya' a coward.' He said 'B'lieve me, soldier, I been right where yer at, an' I know how ya' feel. Truth to tell, I'm kinder nervous myself, an' I ain't no ol' lady."

"Jack," I says, "I feel just like you do."

"Me too," chimed in Thad. "I've been in the bushes four times in less'n an hour."

About midnight, there was still a lot of activity in camp and everyone near us was awake. Sergeant Cates came and got us three, took us off a little way, and said, "I've told the Colonel that ya'll 'er mountain boys an' good shots with a rifle, so you've been temporarily assigned to Cap'n Black's company of sharpshooters an' scouts. Ya'll come on along; I'll take ya' on over there."

We went with him to the edge of the clearing, turned left and continued on along the tree line for near two hundred yards, and turned into the brush. We were introduced to Captain Black who brought out three of the strangest looking rifles we'd ever seen. They had thirty-six inch barrels and were fitted with a brass tube about two and a half feet long on top of the barrel.

He handed them over to us and said, "These are the new sharpshooter's rifles that the navy brought over from England fer us ta use. Them tubes are telescopes, and are good fer four hundred yard shots. Them little knobs on the sides are for windage and elevation. These thangs are sighted in for four hundred yards, so if yer a shootin' closer, ya' have ta aim a little low. If the target's further away, ya' have ta aim a little high. They are forty-five caliber and fire Minie balls."

He held up a ball he took from a pouch and tossed it over to me. It was flat on the backside and rounded in front. "Them pointy ends," the Captain explained, "make the balls fly truer. Ya'll orta use a hunnerd an' twenty 'er a hunnerd an' thirty grains a' powder. See me just before first light, an' I'll tell ya' what I want ya'll ta do. That is all." He turned and walked away.

Sergeant Cates led us back to our gear and gave us some advice. "The Cap'n is gonna put ya'll ta poppin' Yankee officers, as sure as I'm a standin' here. Ya'll will climb trees 'er hide in the brush an' shoot from thar. It don't matter none where ya' shoot from, don't never shoot more than once from any one place. Find yer target, fire an' get out'n thar. Find another tree 'er other position, fire an' move on. Keep in mind that them guns smoke, an' each time ya' shoot, ya' give yer position away, less'n its dark. Keep movin' an' good luck. Oh, an' one more thang. Lissen fer the bugle calls, fer if'n ya' don't, ya' don't know what's a goin' on. Good shootin' boys."

I reckon that ol' man didn't want us a rushin' in and gettin' killed right off. I know he arranged that for us. Funny how some men show concern, ain't it?

We taken our gear and horses over to where our new company had left theirs, and squatted down by the fire to wait until Captain Black sent for us. He had nine other sharpshooters waiting there besides us three. We all sat there a playin' with our new rifles. The first time we would get to fire them would be in a real battle. I wished I could fire the thing a few times before I bet my life on it. Didn't get to, though.

A corporal came and got us at about three in the morning, and took us over to where Captain Black's tent was. He saw us a comin', stood up and motioned for all of us to be seated around the fire. "There's coffee in the pots, boys, help yerselves." He went on, "Smoke if ya' got 'em." He lit a pipe sucked, tamped and relit.

"Some a' ya'll," he continued, "are new to my command, so I'll tell ya' somethin' about us. We're kinda special, in that we ain't too military. All we do is scout around some and pick off Yankee officers, now an' again. Well, it ain't quite that simple, but that's what we do.

In a little bit, Sergeant Bonner will take ya'll ta yer primary positions. Now, what I want ya' to do, I want ya' ta start at first light a pickin' off Union officers whenever ya' can get 'em in yer sights. The ones we want most go like this; a general is always good, but hard to find, fer they don't like the shootin' part much, an' stay away when they can. They 'druther make plans somewheres else. Colonels an' Majors are next, followed by Captains. Always take the highest rankin' officer ya' can see, with one exception. If'n ya' got a choice between a Lieutenant an' a Sergeant. Take the Sergeant. Good Sergeants are worth half a dozen Lieutenants, fer they know the men an' are trusted by them, so they make good targets.

Our job is to make the Union officers the most nervous sonsabitches ever drew breath. Nervous, scared officers make the mistakes that will win this war fer the South.

Now each one of you," he went on, "is an independent unit of force. What that means is that you will use your own judgment as to when to withdraw from a position and set up a new one. If ya' see that our troops are moving in any direction, ya'll are free to move, too. Always try to cover our troops, for their safety and preservation is our main concern. Use yer own judgment as to where to set up. If'n it appears that ya' might be captured, destroy them telescope sights, fer the Yanks'll use 'em on us.

Take all the powder an' lead Minie balls ya' think ya' can use, an' good shootin'." He finished with, "Foller the sergeant, here, an' he'll take ya' ta yer positions. Ain't no use waitin' ta engage, 'cause the Yanks know we're here, an' we know they're there. I'll see ya'll after the fightin's over."

Sergeant Bonner led us off, to stretch twelve sharpshooters the length of the meadow, all along the treeline. Jack was the first of us three to be dropped off, Thad was next, and then me. Four of the others continued on along the treeline. We knew that the sun would be in our eyes when it came up, so we were thankful for the billed caps, called kepis, or forage caps, and for the telescope sights on the rifles. It seemed as though there was a lot depending on us, for there were scads of Yanks out there, from the scout reports we'd heard last night. We surely intended to give them a lesson, come first light, though.

My first taste of war came as the sky lightened to false dawn. I couldn't see the enemy, for the opposite tree line was still in the darkness. I could barely see the treetops against the sky when I started hearing faint popping sounds up and down the line. I knew that the popping sounds were the first gunshots of my first battle, and I knew that the Yanks had fired them. The sun lit our tree line before it did theirs and they were able to see to fire first.

I poured a hundred and twenty grains of black powder down the barrel of my new sharpshooter's rifle and rammed home a Minie ball. I put the hammer at half cock and climbed the tree that was to be my first firing position. I found a crotch in the tree trunk big enough to get comfortable in and sat there and waited. As the light improved, I placed a percussion cap over the nipple of my rifle and scanned the enemy tree line for my first target.

Vision was improving now, and our boys were beginning to fire at the Yankee lines. As the light increased, so did the gunfire, and I was able to pick out individual targets among the enemy. I wasn't real sure how to tell an officer from an enlisted man at that distance in the half light, but I finally saw a man ride up on a horse and wave his arm, motioning to a group of soldiers. When one of the troopers saluted him, I put the crosshairs of my new telescope sight on him, pulled the hammer to full cock and took up the slack in the first trigger.

I felt the faint snap as the first trigger set the hair or firing trigger and slid my finger carefully to the rear trigger. I figured the target to be about four hundred yards away, so I positioned the cross hairs on where I figured his nose to be if I could see his features, took a deep breath, let half of it out, steadied and stroked the rear trigger. I was concentrating so hard, I didn't even hear the rifle go off. I just felt the recoil in my shoulder and put the sight back on the target. I was just in time to see the officer's arms jerk upward and watch him fly off the rear of his mount like he'd been swatted by a giant hand. A spray of blood was still in the air as the troopers on the ground scattered like a bunch of quail. I shinnied down that tree and leaned against it, breathing fast and shaking some.

I had just killed my first Yankee, and at a distance, too. I wasn't real sure how I felt about that, but I didn't have time to worry about it now, so I reloaded, ran to another tree, about thirty yards away and skinned on up in it to try another shot.

The Yankees charged us then, and the fight was on for fair.

We met the charge and you could hear that wild rebel yell as our troops poured out of the trees. The noise and shouting were tremendous, and the powder smoke swirled like fog, obscuring some of the action.

Men and animals were running all over the place and I couldn't tell if the living or the dying were screaming the loudest. I was climbing up trees, firing, climbing down and racing to another tree as fast as I could.

Once, I decided to try two shots from the same tree, and just as I fired the second time, a whole fusillade of balls whistled through the limbs and new foliage, and one of them tore through my new uniform's shoulder pad, only missing me by a hair. I found out then why the sergeant had told us not to stay in one place too long. I had discovered that the Yanks had people just like me, sharpshooters, looking to see my powder smoke and take me right out of the tree. I figured that I might wait a little while, and take out one of theirs.

The battle surged back and forth, but finally found the Confederate forces giving ground. All day long the Confederate forces were pushed back, and I saw so many dead from both sides that I became numb to them. The officers and sergeants I shot all seemed like paper targets after a while. I would fire, and they would fall. Some, but not all of them would just collapse, but some of them would go through awful contortions before they lay still. The smells of battle are even more horrible than the sights; blood and intestines open to the air, besides the smell of the burnt gunpowder.

All day long we were pushed back, and like a fool, I had left my canteen with my gear. I had been so nervous I'd forgotten to bring it, so the only water I'd had was some I took from a dead soldier. I was so tired that I felt like that if I stopped moving, I'd fall asleep and die. My hands and face were black from powder smoke and my throat was raw from yelling and the thirst. As we crossed a little stream, I fell face down and drank. When I got up, I saw a dead soldier and his horse upstream from me, laying in the water. I hadn't noticed 'til then that the water was pink with blood. I threw up, then.

Just at dark, we disengaged, and I went in search of my horse and gear. The horse handlers had kept ol' Red safe, and I got my canteen and drank it dry. We pulled back and consolidated our positions on the west side of the Big Black River to make a stand.

It was real late before I found Thad and Jack, and saw that they were as bad off as I was. We reported in to Captain Black and got our orders for the next day. Four of the sharpshooters we'd been with that morning never did report in. We went back over by the fire and fell asleep on the ground. Many times during the night, we were awakened by screams coming from the surgeon's tent, where some poor soul had a limb amputated. No pain killer, don't you know, as were in retreat and didn't have all our supplies available. We just had to make the best of it.

We were awakened before daybreak and taken to our primary positions again. On the way there, we had to pass the surgeon's tent and the sights and sounds I saw there will stay with me until my own dying day. Bloated, decomposing, smelly bodies were stacked like cordwood, and behind the tent was a pile of arms and feet and legs and hands. Jack puked and I almost did. The surgeons were still working and the poor devils hadn't had a minutes sleep and before long a whole new batch of wounded and maimed would be coming in.

The fighting again was furious. About noon, I wasn't able to climb any more trees or find a place to shoot from, so I had to take to a horse, and ride with the cavalry. The country we had withdrawn to was mostly open, so sharpshooters weren't needed as bad as the troops were. I wasn't riding Red, for he was someplace in the rear. Some of the mounts that were rider-less had been caught up, and the sharpshooters took them to ride. I had taken two Le Mat .44 revolvers off a dead trooper. They each held nine shots, and had a second barrel that took a .65 caliber ball, or you could load it with shot. I also had a sword, as most cavalry men did. We waited in the rear for the next Yankee charge, and I made myself ready for my first mounted engagement. I was so tired I really didn't care if I was killed or not. At least I would rest.

We heard the Yankee bugler blow the charge, and got ready. Our plan was to hit them hard on the flank, and buy our infantry some more time to counter attack. We saw the Yankee cavalry engage our infantry and we hit them in the right flank with everything we had. Captain Black, however, was no J. E. B. Stuart, and we took a lickin'. A bad, bad lickin'. When we closed on the Yanks, we didn't know they had held some cavalry in reserve, and they hit us hard on our own flank, and rolled right over us.

When the Yankees flanked us, I was in the center of our line of battle, and was one of the first to notice the maneuver. The Yankees hit our flank with a crash of gunfire and the sound of screaming horses and men. Jack was nearer the enemy than I was, and I saw his horse go down among a knot of horsemen. Through the confusion of wounded men and horses, I saw my brother regain his feet, and could hear his shrill scream of defiance as he fired into the blue clad enemy horsemen.

Jack had lost his cap and his hair was blowing in the wind. He had his pistol in one hand and a saber in the other and was shooting at men and slashing at horses in an attempt to keep them off him. I spurred towards him, and it seemed like I was riding through all the Union troops in Mississippi. As I neared Jack, I screamed his name and he saw me coming. His face was white under the coating of powder and blood, and his uniform was in tatters. I had forgotten about the Yankees in the effort to reach Jack, and when Jack screamed "Tag!" and pointed his pistol in my direction and fired, I flinched. I was nearly unhorsed by the Yankee trooper that Jack had shot.

The man had been about to crash his horse into my mount to stop me when Jack shot him. His momentum made him fly off his horse and fall into me. I recovered my balance just in time to reach an arm down and snatch Jack up behind me. I spurred the horse, and we broke through the enemy and were temporarily clear of the fight. Our troopers were getting hurt badly and were falling back. Riding double, we circled to the left, got behind our own lines, and stopped a rider-less horse and Jack jumped up on him, caught up the reins, and galloped back toward the fight. I was right behind him.

The fighting went on all day, and when night fell, we moved, under the cover of darkness to positions that we had already prepared in Vicksburg. We had fought as hard as we could, but there were just too many Yankees. We had been defeated twice in two days and were tired and needed time to lick our wounds. We searched and searched, and finally found Thad waiting outside the surgeon's tent, where he had just had a wound closed. He was sure glad to see us.

"I was a hopin' ya'll was alive," he said. "I seen ya' fer a minnit, but you were gone before I could fight my way to ya'."

When we asked how bad he was hurt, he said, "Looks worse'n it is, what with all these bandages. Got a saber cut from the edge of my eye down my cheek to my chin, and on my arm, here. I thought that sucker was a gonna cut my head clean off. Shot 'im right betwixt the eyes, 'fore I fell offa my horse. Somehow er 'nother, ain't nothin' like I thought it was gonna be." That pretty much said it for all of us.

The Yankee Army had us cornered in Vicksburg. We couldn't get out, and they couldn't get in. It was a stand off, just now. We were sure, though that General Joe Johnston would bring his army to the rescue. After all, there was nearly thirty thousand of us holed up in Vicksburg, and he needed us right bad. We just figured to hold off the Yanks a while and take it easy until Johnston got there, and then we'd whip them suckers good.

Ol' Grant ordered an attack on the city on May 19, 1863. You never seen so many soldiers in all your born days. The Yankees was so thick you couldn't hardly miss a shot. We rode out to meet them at first, but we could see that our real defense was to stay put and wait for General Johnston to show up. From where we were, we could get a shot at them, now and then, but they weren't having much luck getting to us.

Our lines held firm, and Grant stalled cold. Three days later, he tried again, and again we managed to beat him back. Grant saw that he would not be able to take Vicksburg by direct assault, so he had no choice but to put the city under siege. We didn't mind too much, for we had lots of supplies, and Johnston wasn't too far away. We held firm.

Some places, the armies weren't no more than a few yards apart. We scouts and sharpshooters were ordered out sometimes to look around, but Grant was not about to leave. That left us sharpshooters to keep the Yankees harassed as much as we could. With our lines so close together, anyone dumb enough to stick his head up got it blowed off. That went for both sides, not just ours.

Tom had made it back to Vicksburg on May 16th, while we were in the field. We didn't find him until the 23rd, after things had let up a little, and we lowly enlisted men were allowed to go into the city for some time off. We were glad to see him and he was sure glad to see us. We found him at the stables, and when we saw him, we all threw our arms around each other and called each other names, and punched each other and grinned ear to ear.

Tom said, "I heared how fierce the fightin' was. I even went down to the Catholic Church and had the ol' priest say a mass fer ya'll. I even lit candles so's ya'll'd be alright. I ain't much fer church goin' but I figgered it couldn't hurt. Anyhow, it 'pears to of worked pretty good, 'cause yer' all here."

We asked how many Yankees he'd seen on his trip, and he said, "More'n I dast count. They's thickern' hair on a houn'. Ain't hardly none of our folks 'tween there an' here."

When we asked if he had any trouble in New Orleans, he told us, "I sneaked in there slicker'n goose grease. Nary-a-soul seen me. I seen my Ma an' give her most o' the gold. Prices are high there. I was afeared ta stay too long, so I tried to leave the very next mornin' but ran into that gambler from the Four Aces. He reckanized me an' I run fer it. Him an' his pal caught me in an alley, an' there was a shoot out. I stole a horse an' hightailed it out'n there. It took a long time to get here, fer I was ascared the Yanks might be lookin' fer me fer the shootin'. I only traveled at night, an' was able to get here 'thout no more trouble. Tag, I'm obliged fer the cut down leather an' the shootin' lessons, fer I'm still walkin' around, an' the gambler an' his sidekick ain't. I owe ya' fer that."

Thad and Jack and I wanted Tom to join up with us, but he said, "Fellers, I love ya'll like brothers, but I ain't cut out ta be no soldier. As soon as them cussed Yankees leave, I'm a goin' back to Texas an' join up with them Morales brothers an' work on buildin' up our ranch. I took that gambler's money, an' now I got enough to put in it. When ya'll get done fightin', come ta Texas, an' see yer ranch. I'll see ya' when yer off duty, and we'll whoop 'er up, but soon as I kin get away, I'm fer Texas."

Time drug on and on. The days passed and everyone wondered where Johnston was. Was he comin', or not? Times were getting pretty tough. By mid-June, a month after we had taken refuge in the city, supplies were exhausted. Nearly thirty thousand troops plus the civilian population had wiped out most of the food stuffs. For the last two weeks, we were reduced to eating mule meat, and were lookin' hard at the horses. I took to sleepin' in the stables with Red. I figured to shoot the man that tried to eat Red

On June 30th, I was called to Captain Black's office. Captain Black had me brought in and told me to take a seat. "Ryan," he said, "I've sent you and that wild brother of yours out more often than I like. You've done your duty well. What I'm about to do and reveal is highly unusual, and could be considered akin to derelection of duty on my part, but here's the situation. I believe that Pemberton will surrender to Grant within the next few days and that being the case, I'm promoting your brother to corporal and you to sergeant, effective immediately. If and when Pemberton surrenders, I don't know what will happen to the troops. I'm hopin' that by making non commissioned officers out of you two, that the Yanks will keep you together. You are too young to be thrown to the wolves in a prison camp. You don't know what happens to young men in prison, but I do. I'm sure you lied about your age, and this is all I can do for you. I've had orders drawn for the three of you to be on a 'special intelligence mission.' That way, I don't have to spell out what you're scouting for. I've dated the orders today, so use them as you see fit. Get on out of here, and live to fight another day, Sergeant. Dismissed."

I stood up and came to attention and saluted. "Thank you, Sir," I said, and I left his office. I went to find the guys, and when I showed them the orders, we sat and sewed on our new stripes. Thad had been made a corporal, too, so he was happy.

We talked it over, and Thad said, "Well, I reckon that's it fer Vicksburg. That'll leave the whole Mississippi River to the

Yankees. What we orta do, we orta get a bunch a' the scouts an' make a break fer it. We c'n ride east an' try an' try ta find another outfit. This'n here's done fer."

We left there then, and went to find the other scouts, and told them what we had learned. Everyone felt the same as Thad did, so we made up a plan to break out. We didn't see any use in waiting around, so we got a couple of dozen of us together, and agreed to do it the next night. We took up a collection, and sent a couple of the men to pay three of the cannoneers to fire their cannon at midnight, and create a lot of confusion to draw the Yanks toward their position. Our reasoning was that when the lines thinned, we'd ride like hell and shoot our way through the enemy lines, then split up and each go our own way. I expect that some would desert, but most would ride east to join up with a new unit.

We went and quietly got our gear together, and packed to leave. We didn't have much, just our arms, bedrolls, canteens and such. We three still had those English sharpshooter's rifles, though, and we wrapped them real careful in cloth, got some dried mule meat, and saddled up. We gathered about three hundred yards from where we figured the cannon to go off, and waited 'til midnight. Sure enough, the cannoneers we paid came through for us in good form. At the stroke of midnight, cannon started going off. Sentries of both armies were taken unawares, and fired some of their rifles, and then the troops were yelling and screaming and running around like there was a real battle goin' on.

Everyone started running towards the cannon fire and shooting, and we still waited. After about three minutes, we put the spurs to the horses, and screaming like demons, charged right through the Yankee lines.

We were yellin' and shootin' anything that moved, all of

them were the enemy, so it didn't make any difference who we shot. Thad and Jack were riding hell for leather on my left side. The rider on my right side took a ball and went off his horse backwards. The horse behind tripped over the body, and went down right in the middle of a bunch of Yankees on foot. It caused attention to be diverted from the rest of us and we spurred harder. I caught the reins of the riderless horse, and took him along. We rode hard 'til morning was about to dawn, and found a place to lay up until dark on Big Black River, where we had been defeated nearly six weeks before.

We found out later that Pemberton had surrendered to Grant on July 4th. Grant had starved us out. He took nearly thirty thousand prisoners, over 170 cannon and sixty thousand muskets and rifles. It was a terrible blow to the south. We also learned that General Joe Johnston couldn't come to our rescue because his troops were green and poorly supplied. They were always on the move and engaged with the enemy, too.

Grant usually opted for unconditional surrender, but in this case, in order to shorten the siege, paroled the men and allowed the officers to keep their side arms and one horse apiece. A lot of the troops honored their parole not to bear arms against the Union anymore, but many found their way to service in other southern units.

General Stonewall Jackson had been killed at Chancellorsville, up in Virginia. He had been fired upon by his own troops by mistake, and wounded so badly that he died in a few days. That had happened while we were penned up in Vicksburg, and was a blow to the south, too; though the battle was considered a southern victory. Gettysburg followed on June third. The Yankees claimed victory for that one, but the fact is that both armies were whipped bad, and Meade let General Lee escape into Virginia with his army mostly intact.

We weren't surprised to find out that the Union was enforcing the Emancipation Proclamation everywhere they went. Free Negroes were everywhere we looked. Many, if not most were starving and there was no more "ol' Massa" to feed or house them.

Almost every plantation we passed was in a sad state of repair. Gardens and lawns were untended, and crops were left unplanted or if planted, not cared for. Yankees left nothing but ruin in their wake. Everywhere we went, black women and girls were offering themselves for prostitution to get money for food.

Traveling at night and holing up in the day time, it took about a month for me and Thad and Jack to get to Chattanooga. The others had split off whenever we found southern detachments, but with our orders, we continued on. We wanted to get farther east before we joined an army. If we were going to be soldiers, we wanted to be where most of the action was, and that was in the east.

We almost made a fatal mistake up near Huntsville, Alabama. We had left our day time hiding place a little too soon, and about ten at night, about an hour after twilight, we stumbled into a Union Patrol, and they were as surprised as we were and there was a sharp, short fight.

Thad had been in the lead, and it was just getting full dark. He had heard a horse blow, and had reined to a halt. I almost rode right into him. About that time, Jack went for his pistol, and Thad charged right into that patrol. I was a little late, not sure of what was going on. Jack fired the first shot, and I put my reins in my teeth and drew both LeMats and spurred old Red right into the middle, firing with both hands. Between us, we dropped all five of them Yankees out of their saddles and rode like hell away from there. It was not for several miles that I noticed that Jack had been shot. He was riding right beside me when he whispered "Tag." and toppled right out of the saddle.

I whistled for Thad to come back, and dismounted to see to Jack. It was dark, and when I touched his tunic, I jerked my hand back, for it was sodden with warm blood. Thad went to his saddlebag and brought his spare long johns, and we ripped them in two and crammed them under Jack's tunic. He had been shot in the chest, and the bullet had gone all the way through.

There was a creek not too far back, and Thad led the horses, and I carried Jack in my arms. When we got back to the creek, Thad found us a tangle of deadfall so we could make a camp, and light a little fire. We hated to make a light at night, not knowing the land, but didn't have much choice. We got some water boiling, and got out the kit we carried. We didn't have much, but we didn't have a surgeon, either, and had to make do. I took Jack's tunic off, and removed the bandages we had made.

Jack was still bleeding freely, so I packed the wounds with tobacco and spider webs that we found in the deadfall. Thad suggested that I sprinkle gun powder over the holes, so I did. Gun powder has sulphur in it, and I remembered what the Morales boys had said about sulphur. We wrapped Jack's wound up real tight and put on some coffee to boil. We figured that if no one had spotted the light or fire smoke by now, coffee wouldn't hurt nothin'.

The bullet had taken Jack high in the left chest, just below the collar bone, and had exited just above his shoulder blade. It made a nasty wound, and bled a lot, but didn't look like it would kill him. It was about an hour before he came to. I reckon that part of it was sheer exhaustion. I had thought I was going to lose my little brother. Pa would have been real aggravated at me, if I'd let Jack die.

When Jack finally came around, the first thing he said was, "Give me a cuppa coffee, durn it. You hawgs would drink it all, and not give a shot up soldier a durned drop."

I said, "Jack, damn yer ornery hide, why didn't ya' say ya' were shot?"

"Well," says he, "I didn't want ya'll a thinkin' I was a dadgummed sissy. I didn't know it was bleedin' so bad, 'til just before I blacked out."

"Jack, ya' damned fool," threw in Thad, "there ain't no sissies hereabouts. We killed men an' we been near killed by other men. We didn't whine when we got licked in a fight, nor when we got hurt. They ain't a sissy in sight. Ain't no Confederate soldier alive done better than we done without actual dyin' an' I got a power of livin' yet to do. We ain't got nothin' to prove to nobody. If'n we was to break down an' commence cryin', I still say there wouldn't be no sissies hereabouts."

"Thad's right," I said. "We ain't got nothin' ta prove. We owe each other our lives, an' we got to take care of each other. Ain't no one else a gonna do it. Fer as I can see, it's just us again' the world 'til we get hooked up with another Confederate Army."

We laid up there for a few days, 'til Jack was strong enough to travel. Thad had scouted the area, and had bought some cornmeal for some silver coins, and I had snared some rabbits. We were awful tired of dried mule meat. We shaped up some tortillas like Luis had shown us and cooked them on a hot, flat rock. Them and rabbit stew wasn't too bad for supper.

It was August 6th before we finally got to Chattanooga. We joined up with General Braxton Bragg's Confederate Army of Tennessee. We rode in about mid morning, and I asked directions to the General's headquarters. We were dirty, and travel stained, and had a pretty good growth of beard on us. We had aged far beyond our years, and the troops took us at face value. We found the General's headquarters, all right, but of course, he was too busy to see us, and his aide tried to make us talk to some infantry lieutenant, but I wouldn't do it.

That smart assed lieutenant put me under arrest and ordered me to wait right there until he went and got the Colonel to come and see about my insubordination. When he came into the room, he took one look at my disheveled condition and asked, "What's goin' on here, Sergeant?"

I came to attention and saluted and said, "With the Colonel's permission, I'm Sergeant Ryan and I and two corporals have rode four hundred and fifty miles from Vicksburg to report intelligence and report for duty. We are trained sharpshooters armed with the English rifles and telescope sights, Sir. We are also trained as scouts, and have been traveling under discretionary orders, Sir."

I handed him the orders, and they sure were dog-eared and dirty. He read them and said, "Lieutenant, see to the comfort of these men, feed them, get them a bath and clean uniforms and have them back here in a hour and a half. I'm pretty sure the General's gonna want ta see 'em. Dismissed." He handed back the orders and returned my salute, and went on out of the office.

Lieutenant "snot nose" got a lot friendlier after that, and said, "Come with me, Sergeant, and we'll get you bathed and fed. While you and your men are washin' up, I'll get some new uniforms. I'll just guess at the sizes, and I'll have a private black your boots, too."

An hour and a half later, on the dot, we were ushered into Major General Braxton Bragg's office. He was a hard looking man with heavy brows and a salt and pepper full beard, trimmed kind of short. He had deep set, piercing eyes, and was altogether a fierce looking man. He was said to be a favorite of Jefferson Davis.

Bragg took a look at us and said, "Let me see them orders, Sergeant, I never heard of a 'discretionary' order in my life." He read every word of the orders and scowled. "This Captain Black surely covered yer backside with these, Sergeant. How come you never hooked up with the nearest friendly force to Vicksburg?"

"General," I answered, "Captain Black was of the opinion that all Confederate Forces in Mississippi and Alabama's western region would soon be compromised. He said to ride east gatherin' information about Yankee troop dispositions and report when I got either here, or to General Johnston. We had been penned up so long in Vicksburg that I didn't know where to find General Johnston, but I knew that you command the Army of Tennessee, and bein' from Tennessee ourselves, it seemed like the right thing to do."

"Sharpshooters and scouts are always welcome on a campaign, Sergeant, and I believe that I have just the job for you. You look too young ta be a sergeant, but I reckon I'll take a chance on ya'. This Captain Black must have had a certain amount of faith in ya' ta give ya' a 'discretionary' order in writing; so I'll leave his orders stand, and temporarily assign you three to my sharpshooter company. Your commander is Captain Judd Mears, and will give ya' lots of work ta do. Report any intelligence to Major Cain, down the hall, and then go on over to your company area. The lieutenant will show you the way. That is all." I saluted the general, and we about faced and went out in the anteroom.

We did stop at Major Cain's office and reported what we'd seen on our travels, and reported the skirmish with the Yank patrol. After that, we went to meet Captain Mears.

Captain Mears was a jolly sort of fellow, not at all military in looks or bearing. He was about five feet-eight inches tall, and pudgy. How he could maintain pudgy with the rigors of two years of war, and missed meals that go along with it was anyone's guess. With black hair and black shiny eyes, he reminded me of the Mexican folks we'd seen down in Texas, and made me wonder how Tom and the Morales boys were doing.

He greeted us with a smile and pointed to a bench that had been pulled up next to the door of his tent. "No inside offices fer sharpshooters an' scouts, nosiree. We all are expected to be tougher than sin an' twice as nasty. 'Sides, we come an' go so often, ain't nobody knows where we are. That lieutenant told me I have inherited a baby sergeant an' two baby corporals that was the best rifle shots in creation, and had been trained by Ol' Daniel Boone, hisself, as scouts. Now, that wouldn't be ya'll, now, would it?"

"Well, Sir," I quipped, "I ain't so sure 'bout that Dan'l Boone part, but I reckon we'll fess up to the rest if ya' ain't too careful 'bout credentials."

"Nope," says he, "I'll take ol' Lucifer an' his demons if I can get 'em. There ain't no steady work fer sharpshooters, mostly, 'til we are ready to go into battle, so I got all my sharpshooters out with the scouts, but I got a few that go on scouts in two's and three's, to keep movements down, and take 'targets of opportunity'. What that means, is that whilst yer spyin' on the enemy, ya' take a pot shot at a high rankin' officers if you can get away clean afterwards. That usually means that you sneak in real close an' take a look at 'em, then sneak back an' take a long shot at 'em. Works right well at makin' 'em nervous. I like my scouts to come back in once or twice a week, to report troop numbers and movements. I also like 'em to take enemy dispatch riders, if they can do it an' get away, an' bring all the papers they're carryin' back to me.

I want to know everything about the enemy. I want to know what regiment, what they are eatin', how many of 'em, an' how much ammunition each man carries. I want to know how many cannon, how much cavalry, how much infantry, an' how the officers are dressed. I want to know the condition of their boots, uniforms, and animals. Ya' cain't think of anything I don't want ta know. Without information, we might as well quit fightin' right now. Ya'll understand what I'm tryin' to say?" We said that we did, and the Captain said, "I'll want you to draw rations fer a week on Friday mornin', an' come an' see me 'bout an hour after sunup. I'll give ya' maps an' an area of operations. Any questions?"

We said we didn't have any, and stood up and saluted, and went off to find someplace to throw our gear, and someplace to have some fun.

We went fishing and laid around for a couple of days, and sold the fish to the officer's mess. Might as well earn a couple of bucks, we figured. Friday, about sunup, we drew our rations, got our gear ready, and met Captain Mears an hour later. He gave us some maps and said, "I want ya' ta make an arc back and forth starting thirty miles north of here. We think the Yanks are a buildin' up fer a push. They would surely like to take Chattanooga, an' we ain't gonna let 'em. Ya'll keep in mind what I told ya' 'bout targets of opportunity. If ya' can pop a Yank officer, or a courier, an' get clean away, do 'er. That's all, an' good huntin'."

On the fifth day, we were on our way back to Chattanooga to report when we found a small patrol with one wagon following a trace southeast, and decided to follow it for a while.

It was not possible to keep the patrol in sight, because the woods were kind of thick; we got nearer, but had to fall back by as much as a half of mile in order not to be spotted by some sharp eyed Yank. We didn't stay on the trace, either, but split up. Thad and Jack rode off in the woods on one side of it, and I took the other side. There was always the chance that the Yanks would lay an ambush for us, so we stayed off the trail.

This way, if they did try to get us, they would be unlikely to get us all at once, and those not caught might be able to come to the rescue of whoever had the bad luck to be captured.

I motioned Thad to ride over to me, and explained what I wanted to do. "Thad," I said in a low voice, "I'm gonna ride on around the patrol an' check the road ahead a ways. You take my place here on this side. I'll be back soon as I can, an' if everything looks good, I aim to take that wagon."

I rode on ahead as fast as I could without making too much noise. I rode away from the trace about a quarter of a mile before I turned parallel with the road again, and rode like mad for about two miles, and cut over to the road and watched a couple of minutes, then rode down the center of the trace toward the oncoming wagon. When I heard talking and the jingle of harness, I melted into the trees and looked for Thad. When I saw him, I waved him over.

"I didn't see nothin' on down the trail, so here's what we're gonna do. You go on over an' tell Jack, an' then you two stay on that side of the trace. I'm gonna cut through the woods an' get in front of 'em, an' I'll wait in the middle of the trail. When you hear me fire, you two open up, an' we'll have 'em in an' "L" crossfire. This way we ain't likely to shoot each other. We're out numbered, so be durn careful."

"You're takin' the danger spot, Tag," said Thad, "you be careful your own self." We shook hands and grinned at each other, and I wheeled my mount and rode to circle in front of the Yank patrol.

I got ahead, and rode over near the road, and tied ol' Red in some bushes off the trace, and walked out into the middle of the road. When I heard the harness jingle, I drew both of those LeMats and stood there, waiting. I remember sweating hard and I sure had to urinate. My throat was dry again, too, and felt covered with dust. My gray uniform was dusty, too. There hadn't been any rains for a spell, and even the tree leaves were dusty here. I guess that was why them Yankees didn't even see me until they were maybe forty feet away.

The Yanks hadn't changed position. There were two riding abreast in front of the wagon, and two abreast behind. Bringing up the rear was a lone dispatch rider. Six in all. When the lead riders saw me standing there, they just reined to a stop, and looked at me for what seemed to be an hour, but in reality, it couldn't have been more than a split second. They clawed at their side arms, and I shot both of them right out of their saddles.

Before the sound of my shots died away, I heard Jack and Thad open up with their rifles first, and I knew that the pair behind the wagon was taken care of. Then I heard pistol shots, and figured that they had gotten the last rider, too. The wagon driver was pointing his pistol at me when Jack shot him in the head from point blank range. I hadn't been able to see him good because of the team between us.

I had rushed my shot on the second man, and he was still alive, as was the dispatch rider. My man was badly wounded, but the dispatch rider had turned, and the ball had shot off the top of his ear, and plowed a furrow in his head just deep enough to knock him senseless without killin' him. We looked in the wagon and got out a little medical kit and doctored them up as best we could. We tied the dispatch rider up to a wagon wheel, and drug the badly wounded man over near him before we did anything else.

Thad got the pouches from the dispatch rider's horse and Jack went through the wagon to take anything we could use. We picked up the piles of papers and stuck anything that looked important into our saddlebags, and got ready to leave.

As we mounted up, the slightly wounded Yank said, "You men aren't going to leave me tied to this wheel, are you?"

Jack replied to him with, "Well, yep, we are. We don't rightly care what happens to ya', Yank."

The soldier said, "If these horses run away, and the wheel starts to turn, I'll be injured."

"You're right as rain," agreed Thad, and shot one of the horses so that it fell in its harness. "I reckon that takes care of that problem, now don't it." He said, "I don't reckon that other'n can run off now. You hadn't orta worry too much 'bout what happens ta ya', Yank, yer friends'll be along directly an' most likely turn ya' loose. Be a man, now, an' quit bellyachin'." We turned and rode off toward Chattanooga.

We camped for the night about halfway to Chattanooga, and looked over some of the things we'd taken. There was lots of mention of troop movements, and a sheaf of orders from General Rosecrans to his field officers telling them to tighten the noose around Chattanooga, which they proposed to attack and take. Jack had found a box of federal currency and a thousand dollars in gold. We decided to turn the gold in and keep the paper, it being easier to carry and hide.

Thad put it this way. "That gold is needed by the south, so I'm fer turnin' it in, but that paper money, now, that ain't nothin' to throw away. If we win the war, we can always use it ta wipe our butts, an' if we lose, we'll have a need fer it fer certain."

We all agreed on that. To this day, I'm not certain of we were thieves or not. Taking from the enemy don't seem like thievery, much, unless you take something from an individual. That's how we looked at it anyhow. Besides, we couldn't be certain the gold made it to the treasury at all. It might have been waylaid along the way.

Chattanooga was a major shipping center, and so was heavily fortified and defended by the South. Rosecrans, the commander of the Army of the Cumberland, decided he would take the city, and over the next few weeks, split his forces into five parts in order to surround it. Due to intelligence like ours that had been gathered, General Bragg knew what was going to happen, so we pulled back to a position over the line in Georgia.

General Bragg intended to attack the Federals and destroy them before Rosecrans could get them back together, and we cornered the first group that he got together at a place in northwestern Georgia, not far from Chattanooga, called Chickamauga Creek.

The country around Chickamauga Creek was rolling hills, with plenty of woods and brush interspersed with some small clearings, and the creek meandered along the bottoms. On September 19, 1863 we engaged the Federal troops and fought from bush to bush and tree to tree. Sometimes we were on one side of the creek, and sometimes on the other side of it. As in other battles, we three had the job of sharpshooting. I don't know how many officers I shot that day. I still wake up sweating, just thinkin' about them. There were bodies of men and horses every few yards, but neither side could get the upper hand the first day.

Now, it was real hot with the warm temperature and the humidity along with the furious activity a battle demands. You would try to get a drink from the creek, but the water was pink, and you didn't dare drink it. The fighting tapered off that night by mutual consent, but the sharpshooters on both sides kept every ones head down. Late, after midnight, General Longstreet brought a lot of reinforcements from the Army of Northern Virginia, and we attacked again at daylight.

As we charged from the brush, I tripped over a dead soldier and fell upon another one. Both corpses were so bloated from the heat that they burst when I fell on them. I was covered with stink and innards. I vomited from the mess, and ran to fall down in the creek. I laid down my rifle, and got down on my knees and scrubbed furiously at the mess that covered me. I had pieces of dead men's skin all over me. I had fluids and bloody tissue in my hair and on my clothes, and in my mouth. I was about to throw up again when a Yank burst through the brush and found me there. He aimed his pistol at me and his trigger finger started to tighten.

I said, "Go ahead. I just don't give a durn right now." I went back to scrubbing.

He stood there deciding whether to kill me or not, and then, all of a sudden, said, "I'm tired of it, too." and sat down on the opposite side of the creek, took out a cheroot and broke it in half, lit both halves, handed one across the creek and said, "Here, have a smoke. It's my last one. Gawd, you smell awful." Then he grinned at me. I grinned back at him, and we both commenced laughing. I told him what had happened to me, and he roared with laughter. I just sat there and smiled, and rested and smoked my half of his cheroot.

We sat there for a few more minutes, and I committed his face to memory. It was the first time I'd seen a Yank as another man, just like me. After we finished our smokes, we both stood looked at each other and stretched out our arms to shake hands. "Keep yer head down, Johnny Reb," said the Yank as we shook.

"Keep your'n down," I answered.

Then we turned and walked off through the brush, each goin' on our separate ways, and back to our separate wars.

As the fighting continued, we started to put a bad hurt on the Federals. Yep, we whupped 'em good. Rosecrans ordered a retreat toward Chattanooga, which put him in a bad position, for the south controlled all the supply routes. Chickamauga Creek was a great victory for the South and I'm right proud to have been a part of it.

General Bragg consolidated our forces in positions on Missionary Ridge and Lookout Mountain, and he didn't see any way the Federals could pry us out of there. We held the high ground, at last. This being the case, the General detached half of the sharpshooters and scouts, and sent us west to reinforce General Nathan Bedford Forrest.

General Forrest commanded a group of fast riding, highly trained and well supplied cavalry. A small force, consisting of only 1500 men, Forrest's raiders were doing a wonderful and masterful job of harassing and defeating Yankees. Forrest had been a slave trader before the war, but had discovered sheer genius at tactics. He was the most famous and successful raider of the war.

The winter of 1863 and 1864 was one of the worst in memory. Almost all the forces were in winter camps and the weather prevented large battles from taking place. We were hungry part of the time, but General Forrest kept us active, reasonably well fed and in generally good fighting trim. We scouts were out constantly. Forrest was not about to be surprised.

Spring brought back renewed activity, and we took the field again. The most memorable battle took place at Fort Pillow, located maybe thirty-five or forty miles up river from Memphis. Fort Pillow was ours early in the war, but the Yankees defeated us and took it in 1862 and had occupied it ever since. We started scouting the area on the quiet about the first of April, 1864, and with our intelligence complete, Forrest ordered the attack on April 12th.

The garrison consisted of about five hundred fifty men. The thing that really made us Southerners mad was the fact that Lincoln had authorized the use of freed Negro troops against the Confederacy. This opened the door for a lot of reported atrocities, what with the Blacks being able to mistreat their former owners. These particular Yankees had trained them as cannoneers. This really chapped Forrest. We all vowed to take that fort back, one way or another.

We attacked on schedule the morning of April 12th and fought savagely for most of the day. We managed to get the fort surrounded, and Forrest decided to be lenient. He sent three officers and me into the fort under a white flag to offer to accept surrender with no further loss of life. The offer was refused and we were run out of the fort at gunpoint. Forrest attacked savagely and immediately.

Nathan Forrest only knew one way to fight; with all his assets and with all his heart. Forrest asked no quarter, and gave none. The defenders tried to fight their way to the river, but we caught them. The fighting was ferocious. The Blacks were afraid to fall into southern hands, and the Whites were too stupid to throw down their arms. When they broke for the river, I took a group of men and cut them off by getting between them and the river. Another sergeant had followed us with some more troops, and saw the chance to form another classic "L". With my men riding toward them from the river, and his men strung along the south side of their route, the carnage was terrible.

I had been riding ol' Red real hard, scouting this area, and didn't ride him into battle today. I was riding another horse, and it sure was lucky for me. As I turned our men back to form a line between the Yanks and the river, just as I ordered the advance, a bullet struck my mount, and when he went down, he pinned me to the ground with his weight. The enemy was coming towards us, and I couldn't get free. The lead was flying hot and heavy, and I was trying to twist around to fire the LeMat with my right hand when a soldier rode between me and the enemy and jumped off his horse and stood his ground, firing with both hands. I saw it was Thad. Another soldier jumped off his horse and took a length of the reins he had cut off my mount's headstall, and tied it to my saddle and to his saddle, and drug that dead animal off of me, jumped back on his horse and spurred after the enemy.

The Yankees finally did surrender, but not until we had killed about two hundred and thirty of them out of five hundred and fifty.

Thad sewed up my hand after packing the holes with some medicine he took from the fort, a needle and a piece of fishing line. "Yer real lucky, Tag," he said, "it musta been a little chunk that went through. Only broke one bone, fer as I can see. We'll tie the palm flat to a little stick and you'll be alright, I guess."

"I'll get the surgeon to take a look at it when he gets free of the bad wounded," I replied. "I owe ya' a bunch fer what ya' done, Thad."

"Don't talk like ya' got shot in the haid, Tag, you'da done it fer me."

Jack finally showed up, and had to check out the wound and make sure I was goin' to live, I reckon. Seemed like I been hanging around with a buncha ol' ladies, for Gawd's sake. Hurt some, but it wasn't nothin', considering.

We spent the next couple of months raiding and doing dirt to the Federals on a regular basis. They just couldn't out figure Forrest. We worked mostly in Northern Mississippi and Southern Tennessee, but sometimes went further away to keep the enemy off balance. We were such a thorn in Sherman's side that he sent Yankee General Samuel Sturgis to find us and put an end to what Sherman called our "depredations".

During the first week in June, Sturgis got together nearly nine thousand troops and came after us. Our corps had grown to about three thousand, give or take a few, and Forrest was complaining that it was becoming unwieldy, and hard to provide provisions for. He was right glad to have so many of us about then, though.

June was awful wet, and it rained constantly. The creeks had overflowed and the roads were nothing but mud. Forrest, that ol' fox, just showed enough of our troops to lure the Yankees out in force. With baggage trains, supplies and even blacksmiths, they were bogged down axle deep in some places. When Forrest had them just where he wanted them, their troops were real close to their wagon train, we attacked and caught them with their pants down. It was at Brice's Cross roads, two days ride south and east of Memphis.

About mid morning on the tenth, the Yanks had been moving in the mud for a few hours, and were having a tough time of it. Their guns were mired down and most of the wagons, too. We had been in position for several hours, and were wet, hungry, and short tempered. We knew we were out numbered three to one, so this was to be another one of Forrest's total efforts.

Even cooks and horse handlers were mounted and armed, and at the signal, which was a shrill whistle, all three thousand of us gave the wild rebel yell and charged. We hit those Federals with everything we had. They tangled up in their own wagon train and couldn't get a counter attack started. Men and animals were screaming and dying, and the wet air was filled with gun smoke. Dead and wounded were to be seen everywhere, and the fighting was going on without regard for stepping on and riding over the fallen. Knots of fierce fighting were the rule of the day.

I saw a large knot of men being surrounded by Yankees, and rallied a dozen troops around me and ordered them to attack and try to rescue our boys. There was a tangle of men and horses and equipment, and the Yanks had our boys two thirds surrounded. Me and my troopers took our reins in our teeth and drew pistols and charged, firing without regard as to Yankee men or horse. Our purpose was to rescue our own, not be kind to animals and unhorsed Yankees.

I lost four of my horsemen before we got to the fight, and three more before we broke through. Jack, Thad, me, and two troopers were all that remained of the thirteen that we started the charge with, and we swept in among the Yankees and killed them in batches.

Their encirclement broken, we were able to ride in at a gallop and each took a Confederate soldier up behind us, and rode on through. We had all been slightly wounded, but none of us survivors were seriously hurt. I rode up to a loose horse and leaned over and grabbed the reins and drug him along side and said over my shoulder, "Mount up, trooper, this fight ain't over yet."

"Yes, Sir, sergeant," the trooper said, and I looked back at him, for no one calls a sergeant "Sir". It was General Forrest, himself. I started to stutter an apology, but Forrest said, "Ryan ain't it?" I said it was, and Forrest said, "Let's go, Ryan. Like ya' said, this fight ain't over yet."

It was dark by now, but we didn't let up on them Yankees. They finally broke and sounded retreat, and we chased and fought them for several miles in the dark. They had left their wagons full of wounded and supplies behind. We found out later that they had lost near two thousand men with being killed, wounded or captured.

Two days after the fight, we had withdrawn to a safe area for rest, and I was summoned to General Forrest's tent. When I got there, I was surprised to find our Company Commander, Captain Fitzhugh, and a couple of other officers already there. I reported to the clerk and was told to wait for a little bit. In a short while, I was ordered into the tent, and the officers followed me in. I came to attention in front of the General's camp table and saluted. He returned the salute and stood.

He leaned over the table and said, "Son, that was a brave thing you an' the other boys done at the Crossroads. My fat was in the fire, for sure, and by your actions I am still a living today. After due consideration, I have decided to give you a direct commission for the sake of expediency, which I am empowered to do according to the articles of war. These officers will attest to this commissioning, and the clerk will give you a formal copy. The original will be forwarded up for permanent record. I am empowered to do this up through the rank of Captain. The two corporals and the privates are to be raised one grade forthwith."

Forrest reached out to shake my hand and said, "Thankee, Captain Ryan. Now that the formalities are over, I'll pour ya' yer first drink as a commissioned officer. This ain't hard liquor, for I don't believe in it." When we each had a shot of lemonade, he continued. "Major Sullivan will help you with a table of equipment and organization. You can keep both of yer sergeant friends with ya'. Little unusual for a company of this size to have two sergeants, but we're a little irregular out here. That's all, Captain Ryan, an' thanks again."

I thanked him again, saluted and left. Major Sullivan fixed me up with a new tunic and a campaign hat, and gave me the stripes for Thad and Jack. As I was looking over the area that I had moved my fifty men to, I thought to myself, "I bet ol' Forrest would dirty his drawers if he knowed he just made a Cap'n outta a seventeen year old kid. Shoot," I thought, "some a' my men had families a' their own when I was still wearin' three cornered pants."

Thad and Jack were glad for me and happy with their new stripes, too. I split my fifty men into two twenty-five man platoons, and put one of my new sergeants in charge of each of them. I called both platoons together and told them I was determined not to let Forrest or ol' Dixie down. I drilled my men 'till I was sure they hated my guts and even Thad and Jack were a lookin' at me funny. When I figured the men had about all they were going to take from me, I called them together again, and made a little talk.

"Reckon you men think I been rougher on ya' than I needed ta be," I began, "an' I 'spect it's so. The reason I have been is this; I been in too many fights an' seen to many of our boys killed from stupidity. I reckon I needed the trainin' worse'n ya'll did, an' I thank ya' fer puttin' up with it. I'll do my best by ya' an' I expect ya'll ta do yer best by me. After seein' ya' work together, I don't reckon we'll be shamed when the General sends us against the Yanks as a company. I ain't never seen a harder bunch than you boys are, an' I'm right proud of ya'. That's all."

At officer's call on June 20th, Forrest explained to me that he was going to cut his forces in half to get back to the light, mobile unit he was so good at fighting with, and said that he'd received permission to send half his forces to Lee up in Virginia, and my company was one of the units to be sent east. In all, fifteen hundred of us were to be sent. We were to leave in small groups of no more than one hundred men, for too large a force would attract unwanted Yankee attention. Our orders were to report to Lee on or before August 1, 1864. We were to ride nearly a thousand miles through the enemy in forty days. We were ordered not to engage the enemy unless we had either numerical superiority, military advantage or unless we had no choice.

Troops were needed so badly in the east, Lee didn't want to waste any on useless battles. I left with my company the next day, with as much ammunition and supplies as could be spared. We were expected to live off the land, or commandeer food and equipment along our route.

Up by Murfreesboro, Jack came in to tell me that some of his scouts had spotted a small Yankee supply train. We were in dire need of food and boots, so I went to take a look at it. We got in position about mid-morning, and I checked to see how it looked. The train was small, as reported, and had only five wagons, and about thirty-five troops with it. One of the wagons had a separate escort of twelve mounted men besides the two on the wagon box. There were six troopers in front of the wagon and six behind. It made me wonder just what they were a guarding.

The way the troops were lined out, the whole wagon train was not more than a hundred yards long, and they must have felt safe, because we didn't find any flankers out. The terrain was hilly, and about two miles ahead, the road went through a kind of pass with hills on either side of it. The whole pass was about three hundred yards, end to end, with a little bend in the middle. We raced ahead and I set my men so that I had one platoon ranged along the whole pass on the hillside above the trace. I split the other platoon and used a dozen men to close the trace and block any escape attempt by the enemy. All the men were well hidden except for me and two others and we were standing in the middle of the road.

The wagon train entered the defile, and I could hear the creak of wheels on ungreased axles and the jingle of harness. As always, my throat was dry. I guess I ain't never going to get used to this. I licked my lips and drew my pistols. When the lead riders saw us standing in the road, they didn't quite know what to do, so while they were deciding, I shot two of them, and gunfire rippled up and down the defile. It was over in about ten seconds. There were twenty-two Yanks killed in the first volley, and the rest threw down their weapons and surrendered. Of the seventeen survivors, only five were not wounded.

Not even a horse got away from us. I didn't lose even one killed, and had only four slightly wounded. My first ambush was a complete success. We sure enough put the fear of God and the Confederate Army into that bunch of Yankees. The survivors wouldn't be so complacent anymore, I bet.

We went and got our horses and rode on in to see what we'd caught. We needed everything. Our boots were worn out, and so was a lot of our horse tack. We needed food and medicine and blankets. The only thing we had a lot of was ammunition and nerve.

I had Thad get a party and go through the wagon that had been guarded so heavily. It happened to be a pay wagon going from Nashville down to Chattanooga to pay the troops. The paymaster was among the dead. That wagon had a strong box full of gold coins and one full of paper money. Now, our troops hadn't been paid for so long they had forgotten they were supposed to be paid. I resolved to fix that situation tonight. I had a pouch made of all the important looking papers we found, and then I had to decide what to do with my prisoners.

I decided to leave the prisoners there, and made the unwounded ones help load the dead in two of the wagons, and the wounded into another. I left them food, medicine and two horses for each wagon. That was it. We left the weapons, but took the powder and ball. Those prisoners would be all right until someone came to find out what happened to them.

That night, I had Thad and Jack divide the money among the troops. They split it all up equally, and when it was all said and done, each man got just over a thousand dollars. We tried to split the money so that each man had some paper and some gold. We saved some money in gold back to buy provisions, for we didn't hold with taking things from civilians without paying for them. It was too much like stealing.

After splitting up the money, my men were in high spirits. Things had been hard for the South. We didn't have enough of anything, and were facing exhaustion. We had been fighting so long with so little that it seemed that we had never been anything but soldiers. Home seemed years away.

One sad thing to Thad and Jack and me was that we would be passing within seventy-five miles of home, and couldn't take the time to go there. Funny how things change when you're forced to grow up. Once, we couldn't wait to leave home, and now, we'd trade our places in heaven just to get to go home for awhile.

We had a couple more encounters with the Yanks in the next three weeks, and successfully ambushed them just as we had learned from Forrest. Finally, on July 28th, we slipped through the Yankee lines and sneaked into Richmond. Lee had left the day before to go the twenty-five miles down to Petersburg to help Beauregard keep the Federals from taking the city. We just cooled our heels in Richmond, and waited for his return. They were successful, and forced Grant to put Petersburg to siege. It would be awhile before the Federals were in a position to seriously threaten Richmond.

We had a lot of skirmishes with Federal troops, but were bottled up in Richmond most of the time and the weeks drug on. In October and November, Sherman had burned his way through Georgia and taken Atlanta, and the whole south was crumbling around us. Between December 10th and the 22nd, Sherman took Savannah.

Early in 1865, the Yankees under Grant, over a hundred thousand of them, had General Lee and fifty thousand of us cornered in Richmond. Things were going to hell all over, and as far as I could see, if God didn't send his angels to the rescue, we were done for. As soon as the roads dried, the fighting would begin, again.

On March 29th, Sheridan was in position to threaten the last stronghold in the south, and Lee tried to save the day by sending General Pickett to still them. Pickett was defeated on April first, and Grant attacked on the second. We fought like demons, but had to withdraw. We tried to get away to the south, but Sheridan got his troops between us and Johnston's army and we couldn't hook up. We knew then that ol' Mr. McKenna had been right. It was all over.

On April seventh, after nightfall, Thad and Jack and I got together and talked over what we should do. We knew that Lee would surrender, and we didn't know what the Yankees would do to us. We decided to wait one more day before we made up our minds. It was nearly too late.

CHAPTER TEN

On April eighth, Grant sent Lee an offer to accept his surrender with honor. That night, Jack said, "Ya'll c'n do what yer' a mind to, but I ain't a gonna surrender to no damned Yankee. I'm a goin' ta Texas." Then he stood up and went to roll his gear. Thad and I looked at each other and went to do the same. We had given it the best we had.

We got our gear together, and wrapped everything that would rattle or jingle with rags, checked our guns, and sneaked out. There was still a war on, and if the Yanks caught us now, we would likely be the last casualties of the war, for we wouldn't be taken alive.

We went real quiet until we saw the Yankee lines, and sneaked around until we thought we had found a weak place, and started to slip through, when we spotted some sentries. We waited and waited, but they weren't walking a post, they were stationary sentries, about fifty feet apart. We could see the glow from their smokes. They were so sure that they had us cornered that they had gotten careless, for no one smokes on guard.

Me and Jack handed our reins over to Thad and went off into the dark, me for one sentry and Jack for another. I went real slow and circled around the one I had chosen, crept up real close, drew my knife, grabbed him from behind and cut his throat. Blood sprayed out in great gouts and I caught his rifle before it hit the ground. He hadn't made a sound above a soft gurgle. By the time I got back to where I'd left Thad and the horses, Jack was already there. We mounted without a sound and sneaked on through the enemy lines and rode like crazy men for a half hour. We knew the Yankees would have found the sentries by now, and we wanted to be well away before the alarm was sounded.

About three o'clock in the morning, it was as black as the inside of a cow. The sky had gotten overcast, and there was no moon to show the way. I wanted to find a place to lay up in the coming daylight and had just turned in my saddle to see if I could make out one of the other boys when the black stillness was shattered by gunfire.

Long lances of flame from the muzzles of the guns streaked toward us, licking at us like tongues of fire from hell. The Devil's own noise filled the night, the crash of the guns, the screaming of men. I didn't know if I was screaming the loudest or not. A tongue of flame licked at my neck and at the top of my shoulder, and I heard a horse scream behind me and the jingle of metal and the creak of overstrained leather as the animal fell. We had let our caution slip for the first time in the war and ridden right into the jaws of an ambush.

As quickly as it had started, the gunfire quit and as I lay where I had fallen from my horse, I could hear the sounds of other horsemen riding away. I knew beyond the shadow of a doubt that I would never forgive myself for not hearing them before they heard us.

I whispered for Thad and for Jack and didn't get an answer. I called a little louder, but all I could hear was the labored breathing of a horse and a slight thrashing as the animal gurgled away its life. The night was so dark that I had to feel my way back to where the others should have been. I was crawling on my hands and knees when I noticed I still had a pistol in my right hand. I checked by feel, and discovered that the gun was empty. I didn't even remember firing. I stuffed the pistol into my tunic and crawled forward.

The smell of blood was so strong that I wanted to gag. My left hand touched a horse's head and I felt my way around him and felt the leg of a man. I didn't know if it was Thad or Jack, but I put my hand over his heart and couldn't feel anything, so I laid my head on his chest and could hear a faint heartbeat. "Thank ya', Jesus," I thought to myself, "don't let him die." My hands were sticky, and I knew there was a hole in him somewhere, so I fumbled around in the dark until I found two entrance wounds and tore strips from my shirt and stuffed them in the holes to slow the bleeding until I could see what I was doing. My neck was on fire, but I didn't seem to be bleeding too bad myself. I figured my sweat was running into the wound to make it burn so bad.

I started to feel around again, to try to locate my brother, for the man I found was too big to be Jack. I heard the horse thrash again, so I moved that way. Soon, I came upon Jack. He was as still as if he was dead, but I heard his heart beating, too.

I started feeling for wounds, and found one in his side, which I plugged with a strip of shirt and then I felt his leg, which was wet and warm. As I felt below the knee, right inside the top of his cavalry boot, I could tell that the boot was full of blood and that the leg was nothing but mush and little pieces of bone that felt like gravel. I knew that my brother was bleeding to death and didn't know what to do. Finally, I took Jack's neckerchief from his neck, rolled it into a tube, tied it around the leg just below the knee, and just above the boot.

I couldn't tie it tight enough to stop the bleeding, so I pulled that empty pistol from inside my tunic, stuck the barrel under the scarf and twisted it as tight as I could. Then I took my own scarf and tied the gun in place. There wasn't another dratted thing I could do for either one of them until it got light enough to see.

I drank from Jack's canteen, for it was too dark for me to find my way back to my own gear. I didn't even know if ol' Red was hurt or not or even where he was. Now and then I could hear Thad moan, but I was afraid to leave Jack. There wasn't anything I could do for either one of them right now anyhow.

I had never been more scared in my life. I lay there in the dark and listened to the dead horse pass gas, and listened to the air in his guts rumble and work. I couldn't smell anything but blood and horse manure. I prayed, then, for the first time I can remember since Ma used to tuck me in at night. I wished she was there right then, for I was sure that I was a gonna cry. Ma had been dead for a long time, but right then I missed her more than I can say. When you're in bad, bad trouble, a feller just sometimes needs his Ma, and I don't give a damn how old ya' are, or how tough you think ya' are. Trust me, when the chips are down and your back is against the wall, you're a layin' there with a mouth full of blood, and feeling like you're about to see your last sunrise, you'll think about your Ma.

At about five in the morning, it started to get light enough to see, there in the woods, and I looked at Jack first. He looked dead. His face was dirty and pale, he was covered with blood, and he hadn't moved since the fight. His leg was a sticking out at a funny angle, and when I tried to straighten it out, it folded at the boot top like there wasn't nothin' there. I went over to check Thad, and found him still out of it, too

There was a bottle of whiskey in Jack's pack, so I got it out to make sure it hadn't been broken. I was a gonna need it later. I knew I had to scout the area before I could make a fire, so I spent the better part of an hour doing that. I found an old dugout in the side of a little bank near a creek that we could set up camp in, for I knew it would be a spell before we moved from this place.

All I found of our attackers was some trails leading out of there. There wasn't anyone else about. I didn't even know if the attackers were Yankees or Confederates. Didn't make no difference, anyway, for what was done was done. I hated to think we might have been shot up by our own side, though. It's always easier to hate the enemy.

By the time I got back, Thad was conscious, but in terrible pain. I explained that I was going to have to move both of them to the dugout, and Thad said, "Just do what ya' gotta do, Tag, we cain't lay out here in the open, an' we ain't gonna live without some care. We been well and truly done up."

I moved Jack first, since he was hurt the worst. I wanted to move him before he came to. His leg was so bad shot up that I had to tie both of his legs together, at the thigh, knee, and ankle. While I was a tyin', blood ran out of his boot. I didn't know what to do, except to try to make him comfortable for as long as he stayed alive. I didn't think he was goin' to live much longer, and my heart was a breaking. I carried him in my arms near a quarter of a mile to that ol' dugout, and laid him inside. The dugout wasn't much, but I'd try to fix it up later. I had to take care of my brother and my friend first.

By the time I got back to get Thad, ol' Red had found his way back to the clearing. He had a furrow cut across his rump, but no more bullet wounds. I put Thad up on him and led him back to the dugout, carrying some of the gear from the dead horse.

After seeing to Thad and checking on Jack, I rode back and got the rest of the gear. I found Thad's horse in the woods, but he was so shot up that I had to put him down. I didn't know the lay of the land well enough, so I was afraid to risk the sound of a shot. I had to cut his throat. I took his gear, too. Now we were in a bad way, what with two badly wounded men and only one horse for me to transport them on.

As soon as I got back to the dugout, I built a little fire and put on some coffee to boil, and put a cinch ring in the coals. I looked over at Thad and handed him the bottle of whiskey. He knew what I had to do to his wounds, so he sucked on that bottle like a calf at his momma's teat. By the time the cinch ring was hot enough, Thad had passed out again, so I took my little knife, heated the blade and dug out the bullets. Then I touched the red hot cinch ring to the wounds.

The smell of burning flesh made me gag. I did the same thing to Jack's bullet wound, and when I seared it he moaned, but did not waken. Damn good thing, too, for when I cut the boot off his left leg, I could see that the leg was all but shot off. It was only hanging there by some meat and skin.

A ball had taken the shin bone right square on and the bone just kinda exploded. A good three inch section was missing, having been broken into little pieces. I dug as many of them out of there as I could, but there wasn't a way n the world to make the bone whole. I knew that by night time, it would be putrid. The thing was already smelling funny. I had to get some help, and in a hurry. I didn't even know which way to go to get help.

I loosened the tie around the leg a little, and the blood just came a squirting out, so I tied it tight again. I didn't know what else to do, so I went out and unsaddled Red. Then I took the little hoof rasp out of the pack, went back in and washed it with whiskey and put it in the fire. I got out Thad's big needle and thread that we had used to mend our clothes and dunked them in the whiskey, too.

I was sick at my stomach from thinking about what I was getting ready to do to my brother, and went outside and puked.

Nothing came up, for we hadn't eaten for a good many hours. I went back inside and washed my hands from a canteen and then rubbed some more of the whiskey on them.

My hands were shaking as I cut the pants leg away and got ready to get down to it. I was crying and my nose was running as I severed the rest of the muscle and cords that kept my brother's leg on. As soon as I had the leg off, I pushed it out of the way and got the hoof rasp out of the fire. Holding it in a rag, I filed away as much of the splintered bone as I could, kind of rounding off the edges. I hadn't even known that there were *two* bones in your lower leg. One big one and a littler one behind and to the side of it.

I stuck my knife in the fire as I looked at the stump and tried to figure out what I ought to do next. When the blade was hot enough, I loosened the ties a little, and wherever the blood was a spurting out, I burned the place 'til it stopped. There were four places where it just squirted. I didn't try to stop the little seepy ones. I cut the skin in kind of a cee shape in the front of the stump and left a flap with a bunch of muscle on it on the backside. Tucking the muscle over the end of the bone for padding, I sewed the muscle to itself to make a solid lump over the raw end of the bone. Then I drew the skin kind of tight around the whole mess and stitched it up with little tiny stitches. I stuck a little piece of hollow straw in the seam so the thing could drain, some, and then released the ties I had put on the leg. Wherever the blood seeped out of the stitches, I touched it with the cinch ring.

Jack was moaning some by then, but he still didn't wake up. I looked over at Thad and saw he was watching me. His eyes were as round as dollars and he breathed, "I never seen such a thing. Ya' think it'll work?"

"I dunno," I replied. "Didn't know what else to do. I had to get it done before he comes to." I thought for a while then said,

"After washin' the muscle with the whiskey, there ain't much left. Jack's gonna need it bad when he wakes up. Ya' reckon ya' can get some down him while I'm gone?"

"Where ya' a goin'?" he asked.

"I gotta find more whiskey 'er some kinda pain killer fer the both a ya'll, an' I don't know how long I'll be gone," I said.

"Be extry careful, Tag," said he, "fer anything happens to ya', why me and' Jack, why, we're screwed. Drag me over there by him. If he comes around, he don't need ta be a seein' that leg. Get it outta here."

I bent to pick up the boot that still had Jack's leg in it, then knelt and started to remove the spur from the boot.

"What ya' a doin that fer?" asked Thad. "Get yer haid outten yer rear, Tag, what's a one laigged man a gonna do with two spurs? Now look'ee here, we're a dependin' on ya'. Ya' cain't be a runnin' around in a daze. Just bury the damn laig sommers an' go get the pain killer. The sooner yer gone, the quicker ya' can get back. We're a dyin' here, an' yer a screwin' 'round with a spur. I swear ta Jesus."

I reckon the whole thing had upset me so I couldn't think, for Thad was a hundred percent right. I picked up the leg and went up the wash a ways and buried it in a hole I cut out of the soil with my knife. Then I mounted ol' Red and rode west. It took about two hours to find a trace that led to a little burg where I bought food, whiskey, linen for bandages and some laudanum.

The storekeeper told me that I shouldn't take too much of the laudanum, for it was made from the opium that the Chinamen smoked, and ya' could get hooked on it. I told him that I didn't give a damn and rode back to the camp.

All the way back, I was scared that Jack might have died while I was gone. I prayed, then, for I didn't know what else to do. I wasn't very good at prayin' so I just talked to God like he was right there. "God," I said, "it's me…Taggart Ryan. Ya' got my Ma up there, I reckon. Now lookit, Sir, I ain't a gonna ask nothin' fer myself, fer I ain't got no right, the way I been a livin' an' a chasin' 'round. *You* know what I mean. This here prayer's fer my brother, Jack. He always looked up to me, kinda, an' now I've gone an' got him hurt. He never would a' been in this fix, it hadn't a been fer me. Thad neither. It's all my fault, I reckon. I was a hopin' that ya' could see yer way clear ta let them boys live, maybe. Take it out on me, if yer a mind to, but please, Sir, don't let 'em die. I never called on ya' when things was a goin' good, nor when we was tired, cold, hungry or hurt, neither. Just do this one thing, an' I won't never ask ya' fer nothin' else. I promise."

The boys were both asleep when I got back, so I made up the camp and started some food a cooking. I had bought a live chicken and some vegetables, so I stewed it up and made some broth for them to drink, fearing that they couldn't keep solid food down. I noticed the rest of the whiskey was gone when I got back, so I knew they had had a time of it.

I was a slippin' around tryin' to be quiet, and like to jumped out of my skin when Thad said, "Gimme some a what ever ya' brought back fer pain. I'm about ta turn sissy on ya'."

I gave him a little laudanum and got a cup of broth for him to drink. "Thank'ee Tag, I needed this. Jack woke up whilst ya' was gone, but I fed him the rest of the whiskey and tolt him to lay quiet, fer he was all shot up. He don't know his laig is gone yet. I don't know how to tell him."

"I don't neither. I reckon we'll cross that crick when we come to it," I replied. I was a dreading it, for I knew he wasn't like to take it too good. I knew I sure as hell wouldn't of.

I went out and gathered some firewood then for I knew that sometime during the night Jack would wake up again, and I didn't know what I'd say to him. I made a pot of coffee and then lay down to try to get a little sleep. I hadn't had any for a good spell now, and I was so tired I could like to cry.

As I lay there on my bedroll, each time I shut my eyes, I saw the muzzle flashes erupt out of the night again, and the crash of gunfire rang in my mind. Then the damn leg would appear. That thing was haunting me more than any of the people I'd shot. In my mind I could see the thing, like it had a life of its own. Just a laying there bleeding. I knew that it would be with me always. My having to do that horrible thing to my own brother.

I wondered, now that it was done, if I'd done the right thing. I tried to imagine my own leg being cut off, and wondered if I wouldn't rather be dead. Being a cripple in our world was going to be hard doin's, and no mistake. I had never been plagued with too many self doubts, but now, I wasn't sure I was man enough to keep my fears to myself, shut my mouth and nurse-maid my brother through what I knew would be the biggest challenge in his life. What I'd done to him would never go away. He couldn't even pretend that it had just been a bad dream. I'd be lucky if he didn't just shoot me out of hand, when he found out that I'd cut his leg off.

Thad was a feeling some better, and was awake a good part of the night, so we talked some, keeping our voices down. He was taking tiny sips of the laudanum now, just enough to keep the pain dulled to a manageable level. I was feeling like the lonesomest s.o.b. in the world, so I was grateful to Thad. 'Bout midnight, Jack started to stir some, so I propped his head on my lap. As he awoke, I gave him some water and spooned him some broth. I told him not to move around too much, and after I gave him some laudanum, he drifted off again. He was a burnin' up with fever, so I spent the rest of the night talking to Thad when he was awake, and wiping down Jack's whole body with cool water.

Jack had messed himself, so I cut off the rest of his clothes and made a pad to put under his hips so's I would be able to clean him up now and again. It was a disgusting thing to do, but I knew I was a going to be his nurse for quite a spell, so I'd just as well get used to it. Besides, he'd done the same for me when that Yankee shot me a thousand years ago, before we got into the war, so I owed him.

At the end of four days, Thad was up and around pretty good, leaning on a stick to hobble around some. He was a helping me with Jack a lot, too. We had kept Jack drugged and asleep most of the time, and with the opium haze in his head from the laudanum, he still didn't know about the leg. I was keeping the leg clean, but on the fourth day, I noticed that it was swollen up and shiny. It was hot to the touch, too, and when I pressed on it a little, Jack groaned, and I could see little beads of pus around my stitches.

I didn't know what to do, so me and Thad talked it over and decided to make a little cut in it and see what happened. Thad was leaning over on one side of Jack to help him hold still, and I washed the stump with whiskey, heated my knife blade and made a quick slice about an inch and a half long right in the reddest part of the tight skin. Stinking, green pus shot out of the cut and hit me and Thad right in the face. Got Thad worse though. I pressed the stump again and more oozed out, so I kept it up until I got all that stuff out and just blood was a coming. Me and Thad sewed up the new cut after dumping some more whiskey in it and just hoped for the best.

The next morning, Thad was a laying on my bedroll, out in front of the fire, and I was on top of the dugout laying pieces of bark and sod to keep the rain from coming in because it smelled like a storm, when Jack awoke with a scream. Thad jumped like he'd been shot again and I slid down the bank and went inside. Jack was half sitting up and bleeding again through the bandages on his chest and staring in horror at the stump of his leg. "Tag, Tag!" he was screaming, "OH! GOD, NO, NOOOOO!" He fell back atop his bedroll and started crying and sobbing.

I sat beside him and lifted and held him in my arms until the sobbing subsided. It took a long time. Finally, he just laid there staring at the roof while I changed all the bandages and tried to talk to him. He wouldn't say a word to me, so I had Thad try. Jack wouldn't talk to him, neither.

Thad or I one was with Jack all the rest of the day. He wouldn't take no water or food neither one. Finally, 'bout sundown, I said, "Jack, ya' gotta eat somethin', even if ya' don't feel like it."

"Tag," he croaked, "I don't have ta do nothin'." That's all he said 'til me and Thad turned in for the night. In the middle of the night, I heard Thad swear, and awoke just in time to see him grab Jack's hand and pull a pistol barrel out of Jack's mouth. Thad had grabbed the pistol just as Jack had pulled the trigger, and the pistol's hammer fell on the web between Thad's thumb and forefinger. His hand was bleeding right fierce. He was awake and saw Jack put the pistol in his mouth, and grabbed the gun just a split second before my brother blew his brains all over the dugout.

"Jack," I said, "what ya' wanna do that fer?"

"I decided I cain't live as no cripple," he answered, "only part of a man. Not ridin' 'er even able ta walk behint a durn mule an' plow.'

"They's a whole lot worse things than losin' a part of a leg," put in Thad. "Why ya' ain't blinded nor armless 'er nothin. Onliest thang wrong with you, is you'll have ta get a wooden laig, like a pirate, an' stitch a cup onta yer saddle ta be able ta ride. Jesus wept, Jack, don't be a ol' lady."

"Thad's right," I said. "The war's over fer us, an' we can go home, now. Chrissake, ya' ain't a real cripple, ya' only got a little inconvenience."

Then came the part I'd been dreading. "Who done it?" Jack

demanded. "Which one a' ya'll decided ta play God an' cut my laig off?"

"I done it," said Thad.

"No, he never," I put in. "I done it myself. Ya' was a bleedin like a stuck hawg an' the leg was all but blowed clean off. I done it, an' I'd do it again. I just couldn't let ya' die."

Well, we had a real go around about it for a few days, and Jack swore that if I ever told him what to do, or laid another hand on him as long as he lived, he'd kill me sure. I don't guess I blame him fer feelin' that way. It hurt me some, I'll admit, but it don't hurt as bad as it does to see him a tryin' ta move around without a leg. It would a' hurt lots more to just let him die, without even trying to do something. At least God heard me out, and let Jack live. Even if he stays mad at me always, it's better than having him dead. He don't see it thataway, but that's the way it is.

By the end of the second week, Jack was a hoppin' around the camp a leaning on a hickory staff I'd found. He still wasn't saying much to me though. Thad had found a hickory limb about two feet long, with a big knob on one end and he just set around mostly a whittling on the thing. I made another trip into town, bought two saddle horses and a pack horse and some clothes and food. We weren't doing too bad really, out in the woods. We were just a waiting for the boys to heal enough to go home.

We camped there for nigh onto six weeks before we started talking about pushing on. The guys were doing real good, and we had all gained some weight back. We'd all gotten real skinny there toward the end of the war. The Confederate Army just didn't have enough food for men to get fat on.

Thad finally showed me what he'd been a whittling on, and I was real surprised. He had carved most of a wooden leg out of that hickory limb, and had carved a socket in that knot that would fit Jack's stump. While Jack was doped up, Thad had taken some measurements and told me what he wanted me to do.

He had me take the wooden leg into town and get a smithy to make a place to fit a hinge that would allow a little movement to the artificial foot he'd carved. Then, on Thad's instructions, I took the whole thing to a saddle maker who padded the inside of the cup with soft leather and made a thing like a trouser leg that came up to Jack's crotch, and then up the side where it attached to a strap that went around the waist and one that went up over the right shoulder.

I could see that Thad had spent considerable time thinking this thing through. I bought Jack another pair of boots and had the saddle maker split the left one down the back, stretch it around the artificial foot and stitch the boot up again. It looked kind of like a half a pair of pants, with the hickory leg and the boot attached.

What with the limited movement built into the ankle hinge, I didn't see any reason why it wouldn't work real fine. It all depended on Jack's attitude when he saw the thing.

It was coming on to dark when I got back to the dugout, and Jack was asleep again, which made it easier to show Thad the contraption. With any luck atall, Jack would wear it. If he didn't, we hadn't lost anything but a little time.

Lots of nights, Jack would wake up drenched in sweat and screaming. Nightmares, I reckon. I had 'em sometimes, too, but nothing like his. I just woke in a panic, a reaching for my pistol. Thad didn't sleep too well, neither. I reckon war ain't too good for young folks. It kills something in ya' and makes a good time hard to enjoy. Makes ya' kinda moody, too, don't ya' know, what with the dreams and all.

Seems to me that the old fellers that start the wars ain't the ones that have to fight 'em and die or to have them dratted dreams, neither. They don't always happen at night, neither.

Sometimes they flash into your head in broad daylight and take you unawares. It leaves ya' kinda sick at your stomach, too. If you ain't been to war, I don't reckon you can understand.

It ain't just the soldiers that have a hard time of it, for there's lots of non-combatants, like nurses and such, who work with the maimed, wounded and dying that work and live in a horror all their own. Some folks never do get over it. It's a sad but true thing that most of the casualties of war happen after the shooting stops. The horrors of the mind will live as long as you do. Maybe that's the worst kind of casualty. I hope to God that I ain't one of 'em. I been shot, I been scared, I been cold and I been hungry. I been so tired I could cry, but a feller gets over that kind of thing. When you been wounded in your mind, it don't never go away. I'm afeared that Jack's been wounded in his mind.

Like I said, we laid up in that dugout for about six weeks, give or take, before the boys felt like tryin' to move on. Jack wouldn't even try on his wooden leg for quite a spell, saying that it would hurt his stump, and I reckon that it would have. I think the whole thing was made more horrible yet for him just to have to look at that contraption. Finally, during that last week we stayed there, he wore it, and hobbled around on the wooden leg, carrying a staff for a cane.

At first he would turn white from pain, and the stump would be leaking a little blood when he took the contraption off. He finally pulled an old sock up over the stump, and that held down the chafing some. I think the reason he started wearing the artificial limb at all was that he didn't want folks to see him as a cripple. I don't think he wanted anybody to see him atall. Ahorseback, no one would know, and if folks saw him a walking with a staff, they wouldn't know his leg was gone. He didn't want folks to think he was useless, don't ya' see?

Horseback riding was a terrible ordeal for Jack, and Thad wasn't all that strong, neither, when we lit out for home. The first few days, we only made a few miles, increasing each day's ride as they got stronger. It took us a solid month to get home, and it was less than five hundred miles. 'Course, we kept to ourselves most of the time, for you got to remember that we ran off before the surrender, and didn't find out 'til later that Lee had surrendered the next day, April ninth, 1865. It just took us that long to sneak that far.

We kept to the hills when we could, and traveled at night. Almost every plantation we saw, and most of the farms were devastated. Burned, abandoned or just plain gone to ruin. It was a sight to break your heart.

It was a warm day at the last week of June when we turned into the lane leading to our home. We were kind of nervous and kind of excited at the same time. We didn't know what we'd find when we got there, and hoped everything was all right. It appeared that nothing had changed around here, at least on the surface. Red Boiling Springs didn't have any strategic value, and it didn't look like there had been any major fighting around here, either.

We came to Thad's place first, and turned in at the gate. We sat our saddles in front of the house and didn't get down. I don't know why, we just didn't. We just sat there and looked.

Pretty soon an old hound dog came around the corner of the house and commenced barking. That brought Thad's Ma to the window, and she looked out and saw us. She came slowly out on the porch and said in a small voice, "Thad, is that you, son?" And then she screamed, "Thad, Jack, and Tag! John, John," she screamed, "Thad's back!" and she came running towards us. Thad jumped off his horse and grabbed his Ma up and swung her around. They were both laughing and crying at the same time. I hadn't seen Thad shed a tear all through the war, but he did now. It brought a lump to my throat, and I looked over to see Jack wiping his eyes, too. We got down and hugged Thad's Ma, too. She had taken care of Jack and me when our Ma died, and we loved her.

Thad's Pa, John, came a running then, and he hugged us all. "Thank the good Lord ya'll made it home safe," he cried. "Come in an' set, an' talk to us." Jack and I begged off. We were a wanting to see our own place and see our own Pa.

Jack and I mounted up and walked the horses on down the lane. We didn't want to hurry, for we wanted to savor the homecoming. We was glad to be home. We saw Pa down at the barn unhitching the team as soon as we turned in our gate. He noticed us, and just stared as we turned and rode in. He noticed us, and just stood and stared as we rode up and got down. He walked up to us and stood looking at us, and we could see his Adam's apple bobbing up and down like he was trying to swaller. He said, "Lord!" and threw his arms around us and hugged us to him. None of us could say anything right then, so we just stood there hugging each other and pounding each other on the back.

Finally, Pa stood back and with his hands on our arms, he said, "Lemme look at ya'. Goddam, yer' men growed. Ya' look fit an' hard, boys, yer a sight fer sore eyes. Come an' set, an' tell me where ya' been an' what ya' done. One thing first, though, come in the barn an' lets us have a drink a' corn an' they's somethin' I gotta tell ya'."

We went on in the barn, and Pa got a jug and pulled the corn cob stopper and tilted it over his arm and drank, and handed the jug to me. I did the same, and handed the jug to Jack, who drank and gave the jug back to Pa.

Pa took another drink and passed the jug to me and said, "I got ta' tell ya' boys, I been a dreadin' it, but I got it ta do. I married Katie Ball whilst ya'll was gone. I hope ya' don't take it bad. I loved yer Ma, but she's been dead a good while, now."

I tipped up that jug and handed it on to Jack, and said, "Pa, I cain't think of any better news."

"You bet, Pa," says Jack, "she's a fine woman. I'm happy fer ya'. Right proud of ya', too. She's a great lookin' woman, an' I didn't know ya' had it in ya'."

"Wal, I'm glad ya' approve boys, but tell me; Thad is still a livin' ain't he? I see he ain't with ya'," Pa said.

I answered, "Yep, Pa, he's fine as frog hair, an' with his Ma right now, but I 'spect he'll be along after he hears the news."

"Come on in the house, boys, I know Katie will be right excited ta see ya'."

Thad and his folks showed up about an hour later, and stayed for supper. We sat out on the porch and talked 'way into the night, telling all that had happened to us, glossing over the worst parts for the women's sake, but the men could read between the lines on that. Gawd, but it was good to be home. The women finally went in the house, and we men sat there on the porch in that warm June night air and drank corn whiskey and smoked our pipes and talked 'til dawn.

Jack told his own tale 'bout losin' his leg. Like to broke all our hearts to hear him tell of it. Thing of it is, everyone was too polite to mention the limp or anything, figuring it was Jack's own business, and if he wanted to talk about it he would.

Jack never made out like he was a lookin' for sympathy, or nothin'. He just flat out told what had happened as far as he knew it, him being unconscious a good part of the time. Me and Thad filled in the story where Jack couldn't. He never let on that he blamed me for making a cripple out of him, or even that he had hard feelin's toward me. Matter of fact, he had the folks a feelin' sorry for me, a havin' to cut off the leg and all.

We told all the funniest stories of the things we'd done and been through. They didn't need to know how truly horrible the overall experiences were. We wanted to spare them that.

They were pleased to hear that we'd left that money with ol' Nigel Reddington, though. Pa opined that money left with them British shipping companies was bound to double every year, barring ships being lost at sea. We were kind of glad to know that, for where we planned to go, we'd need all the coin we could get.

The ranch and the Morales boys really got their attention. Catchin' wild cattle to sell wasn't anything that mountain folk would have thought of in a hundred years. We told of our dreams and our plans for Texas, and they allowed as how it was a right fine idea. There wasn't much opportunity around Red Boiling Springs anymore, and we would be restless soon, so our folks thought a wild place like Texas would be good for us.

The way they put it was "Ya'll got the kid knocked out of ya' purty young, an' ya'll need room ta grow 'thout no one a lookin' outen the corner a' their eye at yer wild ways. Go on out whar it's wild an' free, an' be true to yore own selves. Do what ya' wanna do whilst ya' can. It's good ta see ya'll well an' strong, even if ya' are as scarred up as three ol' tomcats. Thank Gawd ya' made 'er through all right. Welcome home, boys."

Jack and I helped Pa do the chores and bring in some firewood, and I spent an hour or so chopping wood and kindling for Katie. I still wanted to call her "Miss Ball," but that wouldn't do, now. She looked at Jack and me and Thad a lot. She said, "I've never, in all my born days, seen eighteen year old boys lookin' like old men. Your faces are drawn but that's not what bothers me; it's your eyes. They look a hundred years old, and you are all jumpy. Tag, I've seen you go for your gun when the door slammed. You boys are never without your guns, and I guess I don't know you anymore. You've seen too much, too fast and too young and it breaks my heart."

"We'll get over it, Katie," I said. "After a while without worryin' 'bout Yanks an' we'll be right as rain." I didn't know then that some of it would stay with us always. A lot of times in the middle of the night, we would awake suddenly, with our guts in a knot and panic in our hearts. It would never go completely away.

Jack and I had taken to sleeping out in the barn or in the open woods a lot. Pa asked us about it and I said, "Pa, we just cain't seem to sleep indoors. We just cain't stand to be cooped up. We been outdoors too long, I reckon, an' we ain't house broke no more."

"I understand, son," Pa says. "I remember how it was when I came home from my war. I was wild as a March hare, an' I reckon if it hadn't been fer' yer Ma, I might not have been house broke ever again."

"Pa," I said, "me an' Jack, I reckon we'll head out fer Texas tomorra'. We been home a month, now an' it's been good, but I reckon we got to get gone. We don't have to worry 'bout home no more, now we've seen ya'. I reckon we ain't cut out fer farmin' no more. We're too durn spooky to stay put in one place too long. We got ta go."

"I know, son," Pa said, "just you remember that this here's yer home, an' will always be here fer ya' I seen to it that it would always be yer home, an' cared fer. When yer ready, now or twenty years or fifty years from now, yer home will be here when yer ready. I got ta thinkin' after ya' was gone in '62, that there was somethin' I never told ya', son. I love ya', an' I'm proud of ya'."

I teared all up, then and threw my arms around him and said, "I love you, too, Pa." I turned him loose and said, "Now don't you go tellin' Jack I turned sissy, hear?" He smiled then and replied,

"All right, son; I promised your brother the same thing." Then he put his arm around my shoulder, and we walked to the house. We'd never been this close to one another.

Jack and I got our gear together to go once again. I took the camphor box I had made, and carefully folded and put away my uniform. I cleaned and put those LeMat revolvers and my commission papers in there, too. After I threw my 'discretionary' orders in, I tossed in my old campaign hat and a tattered old battle flag that I'd carried in my saddlebags. Then I nailed the box shut. That part of my life was over, but I just couldn't throw that stuff away. Lots of hard earned memories were sealed in that box. I figured to ask Pa to save it for me. I wrote Pa a note, and left it with the box.

As Jack and I rode out early the next morning, the last sight we had of home was that of Pa standing on the porch, holding Katie's hand and waving to us. It felt sad to leave again, but good to know Pa had someone.

We picked up Thad up at the gate of his place, and turned the horses west. We didn't know how well we'd do in Texas, but it did feel good to be out in the open again. It felt strange to be riding down the road instead of slipping through the bushes trying not to be seen. We found ourselves wanting to avoid oncoming horsemen. No reason to hide anymore, but we just felt awful exposed.

Pa had tried to give us money from his Mexican gold stash, but we told him that we had plenty of coin, and would be obliged if he'd just put his gold up. We figured that it wouldn't be long 'til the Federals came around, and he might need it. We didn't know how much of it he had, and it was bad manners to ask about a man's money.

We saw Yankee patrols now and again, but we made a special effort to avoid them. We just weren't ready to forget and forgive, yet. Something beautiful died with the war and Ol' Mr. McKenna was right as rain. I'm glad we did what we did, but I ain't sure I would do it again. Ain't sure I wouldn't, neither.

We saw an army of ragged, hard eyed, soft voiced men on our way to Texas. A lot of Confederate veterans didn't have a home left to come home to, and many of the families were displaced. There wasn't much work to be had, so the south was full of drifters. Very few of them had any money, so I was glad to have taken the cash from that Yankee wagon and given it to my men. At least they had some money for a new start. Most of the others were wandering around like lost souls, hollow eyed and gaunt.

I reckon they *were* lost souls. Their pasts were gone, and their futures were looking dim. They were rootless, and many of them were headed west, same as us. All the veterans walked softly around each other, for to give any sort of offence was to have to fight. A man could get killed real easy, offending men who had just spent four years of their lives killing people up close and personal. You didn't run off at the mouth if you weren't looking to fight. It grew to be kind of a code. You didn't lie, you didn't cuss a man and you didn't run from a fight. Your word was your bond. It was a hard way to live, but we were hard men in a hard land.

I will always treasure in my heart something Jack said to me as we rode through our gate on the way to Texas. He said, "Tag, ya' know all them thangs I said in that dugout, 'bout shootin' ya' an' all? I didn't mean 'em. Thank ya'."

As we rode to the edge of a town a day later, we three heard some soft singing. A man sat on the front porch of a little shack. Blind, he was, with terrible scars on his face. He was wearing a tattered grey uniform and forage cap. There were corporal's stripes on the arms of his tunic. As he strummed an old banjo, he sang in a clear, soft voice. Very slowly, he sang "Dixie's Land." I had never heard it sung or played slowly before, and it was the saddest song I ever heard. It brought home to us all that was lost and gone forever.

I hope that someday, when I die, they'll play that song real slow over my battle flag draped coffin.

Oh, I don't want folks to cry for me, but when they get to the part that says "Look away...Look away...Look away...Dixieland"...maybe they'll cry for Dixie.

THE END

Printed in the United States
54908LVS00002B/310-327